The sight sent a jolt of fear through her.

"He's back." Lacey pointed at the snowmobile on the mountain. "And he has a rifle."

As they took cover in a snowdrift, Lacey pushed aside the panic that filled her.

Jude faced her, but neither of them dared make a sound. They listened to the snowmobile grow closer. Just a few more minutes and it'd be past them.

She looked up and her breath caught. "He has her! He has the girl!"

"The roads must be open. He's taking her out of here." Jude reached for his gun. "We have to stop him." He fired a shot.

He jerked his head to one side. Before she even had time to look up the mountain to whatever had alarmed him, a thundering roar surrounded her.

Avalanche.

They bolted downhill but couldn't outrun the wave of snow. In seconds, her body was picked up and tossed around. Snow cascaded around her, enveloping her, and stole her last breath.

Ever since she found the Nancy Drew books with the pink covers in her country school library, **Sharon Dunn** has loved mystery and suspense. Most of her books take place in Montana, where she lives with three nearly grown children and a hyper border collie. She lost her beloved husband of twenty-seven years to cancer in 2014. When she isn't writing, she loves to hike surrounded by God's beauty.

Books by Sharon Dunn

Love Inspired Suspense

Dead Ringer
Night Prey
Her Guardian
Broken Trust
Zero Visibility
Montana Standoff
Top Secret Identity
Wilderness Target
Cold Case Justice
Mistaken Target
Fatal Vendetta
Big Sky Showdown
Hidden Away
In Too Deep
Wilderness Secrets
Mountain Captive

True Blue K-9 Unit

Courage Under Fire

Visit the Author Profile page at Harlequin.com for more titles.

MOUNTAIN CAPTIVE

SHARON DUNN

LOVE INSPIRED SUSPENSE
INSPIRATIONAL ROMANCE

LOVE INSPIRED® SUSPENSE
INSPIRATIONAL ROMANCE

ISBN-13: 978-1-335-72158-7

Recycling programs
for this product may
not exist in your area.

Mountain Captive

Love Inspired
22 Adelaide St. West, 40th Floor
Toronto, Ontario M5H 4E3, Canada
www.Harlequin.com

Printed in U.S.A.

Weeping may endure for a night,
but joy cometh in the morning.
–Psalm 30:5

I cried by reason of mine affliction unto the Lord, and
he heard me; out of the belly of hell cried I, and thou
heardest my voice. For thou hadst cast me into the
deep, in the midst of the seas; and floods compassed me
about: all thy billows and thy waves passed over me.
–Jonah 2:2-3

For Shannon, who brings so much humor and adventure into my life. So glad you are my son.

ONE

Private Investigator Jude Trainor gripped the steering wheel of his SUV as it hugged the upward side of the narrow mountain road. One small overcorrection and he ran the risk of sailing off the road and down the steep incline. Windshield wipers beat out an intense rhythm, wiping away the increasing snowfall. The radio forecast an unexpected blizzard, the worst Montana had seen in fifty years.

He could just make out the red taillights of the car he'd chased for miles. The car matched the description of the one believed to have been used to kidnap an eight-year-old girl over a week ago from her home in North Dakota. There was no way to match it to the driver because it had been reported as stolen a day before the kidnapping.

Was the girl being held in a remote cabin in these mountains? Jude doubted the suspect would lead him to the girl. What he hoped for was to take the driver into custody and get him to confess. But the driver had not stopped when they were on the highway. Now with only the two of them on this road, he must know he was being tailed. Jude prayed for an opportunity to stop or disable the car.

The car had surfaced around various parts of Montana, but this was the closest Jude had gotten to the suspect.

The road curved and the red taillights disappeared.

Snow cut Jude's visibility. He let up on the gas until he was moving at a crawl. Wipers cleared his windshield only to have it fill up again with snow. All he saw was white everywhere. The car couldn't have gotten that far ahead of him. The wind blew with such force, he could barely make out the tracks where the other car had been.

Headlights filled his field of vision. Adrenaline flooded his body. The other car had gotten turned around and was headed straight toward him on the one-lane road. He tensed, ready for a fight for his life.

Jude shifted into Reverse. He drove more by feel and instinct than by what he could see in his mirrors. His car hugged the upward side of the road.

Through the snowfall, all he saw was the

glowing orange of the headlights as they loomed ever closer to him. He prayed for some sort of shoulder to pull off on. Bushes scratched the driver's side window because he was so close to the bank.

Though the other car was moving at a crawl as well, it closed the distance between them.

He checked his mirrors and then craned his neck. The snowfall cleared for a moment, so he had a view of the road. He couldn't see a safe place to pull over. He pressed the gas even harder, guessing at where the safest route was.

He felt a thud against his front bumper.

He set his jaw and gripped the wheel. No, this could not be happening. He was not going over that incline.

Jude shifted into First. He revved the engine and pushed toward the other car, which was only a few feet away. If this guy wanted to play demolition derby, bring it on.

The other driver backed away a few feet. Jude brushed his hand over the gun in his shoulder holster. For the kidnapped girl, he needed the suspect brought in ready to talk. Even if he injured him to capture him, it meant a delay in finding the child.

An idea struck him. He turned off his headlights and continued to back down the mountain.

The other car backed away, as well. Now he saw the flaw in his plan. The guy would back up until he got to the place where he was able to turn around and then take off. With his lights still off, Jude edged forward. The headlights of the other car faded in and out as an intense wind gusted.

They came to a straight part of the road. The other car barreled toward him at a dangerous speed. He hit Reverse again. His windshield filled with blinding yellow light right before metal crashed against metal. The whole car seemed to be vibrating and creaking. His back end fishtailed. And then he was sliding sideways. His hand gripped the wheel. He pumped the brake. The car slipped off the edge of the road. He felt weightless as the seat belt dug into his chest and the car rolled twice before coming to a stop right side up.

The crash had taken the wind out of him. Still numb, he unclicked his seat belt. His door was too bent to open. Though he was in pain, he didn't think he'd broken anything.

He pulled his phone out. No signal.

Jude dragged himself toward the passenger side door. He clicked the handle and pushed it open. A gust of snow chilled his face as he crawled out.

He heard the zing of the rifle shot before

he heard it hit the metal of his wrecked vehicle. His heart pounded. He could just make out the silhouette of the possible kidnapper standing in the headlights of his car, aiming a rifle down the mountain at him.

Adrenaline surged through Jude's body as he crawled around to the front of his car for cover. His bright colored ski jacket would be easy to spot even in the storm.

The freezing cold enveloped him. He'd kept his winter coat on, but he had no hat or gloves. He wrestled with the thought that he might die out here. That his life would come to nothing. And that the little girl would not be brought home safe. That bothered him more than the reality of his own death.

Another shot rang through the air. Glass shattered.

The possibility of bringing that little girl home safe to her parents had felt like a shot at redemption to him. He wasn't a private investigator by choice. At the age of twenty-one, ten years ago, he'd washed up as a rookie officer when a domestic call he'd been sent on had ended in the murder-suicide of husband and wife. Their ten-year-old daughter had witnessed the crime. The last he'd heard she was under a psychiatrist's care. Her life would never be the same. The guilt weighed on him every day.

If only Jude had said the right words as he'd talked to the husband through the open window. If only he'd chosen a different tactic. If only...

Jude peered around the side of his car. The man with the rifle was nothing more than a dark spot, but he was still there waiting to take another shot at Jude.

The cold seeped into his muscles as he wondered if he had the strength to make a run for it into the unknown down the mountain. The winding road was the one he'd just come up in his pursuit. Maybe there was somebody down there, a hunter perhaps. For the first time in ten years, he said a quick and desperate prayer.

Lord, send help or show me a way out of this.

Wildlife biologist Lacey Conrad put the binoculars up to her eyes and scanned the winter landscape until her view landed on a ridge where she expected to see elk appear within the next hour. She gripped the binoculars a little tighter. She wasn't going to see anything with the storm moving in. Not a good day for research and observation. She let the binoculars fall around her neck. Even on days like this, she loved her job. She preferred being outside and the research allowed her to move around Montana. Since the death of her parents and little brother in a car crash when she was in college, she had lived like a nomad, never putting down roots anywhere. That was the way she liked it.

The wind died down for a moment and movement much closer to her caught her attention. On the mountain road above her, a car had rolled off the road. She'd heard the muffled sound of a crash only moments before. Now as the wind died down, the noise made sense.

She saw a man crouched in front of the car. Her heart squeezed tight. A man holding a rifle was headed down the steep incline. She'd thought the shots she heard before were from a hunter somewhere on the mountain.

The man by the car bolted to his feet. She could see the bright colors of his ski jacket even when the wind picked up. Panic filled her body. It was the man in the ski jacket who was being hunted. The man must have seen the orange of her hunting vest. He made a beeline toward her.

Another shot was fired. The man in the ski jacket fell in the snow. Her heart lurched. Had he been hit?

She ran toward him. Her boots sank into the snow. She looked up the mountain seeing only white. The neutral colors the man with the rifle wore made it harder to see him.

The man in the ski jacket got to his feet. She ran toward him, nearly crashing into him.

He gripped her arm. The fear she saw in his face turned to relief.

A thousand questions raged through her head. Was this some sort of drug deal or other crime gone bad? Was she helping a criminal? Was the man shooting at a hunter who had lost his marbles?

Another shot rang through the air. She scanned the landscape in the general direction the shot had come from, but she could see nothing through the blowing snowfall.

The man in the ski jacket would have to explain later.

The only thing that was clear to her was that his life was in danger.

She tugged on his sleeve. "This way." Her truck was parked down the mountain in a grove of trees.

They half ran and half slid down the mountain toward the next section of winding road. She hurried through the evergreens to her truck. She yanked open the driver's side door.

The man in the ski jacket got into the passenger side of the truck.

She glanced over at the stranger sitting across from her. Her heart was still racing from running from the shooter.

He met her gaze. His eyes looked honest, anyway. "Thank you," he said. "You saved my life." He was still trying to catch his breath.

She wasn't sure what to think about this stranger. She pulled through the trees and out onto the road. The heavy snowfall on the un-plowed road meant she had to go slow. "I'll take you as far as Lodgepole where I'm staying. There's no law enforcement there. Tiny town, only two hundred people." Her voice dropped half an octave. "Obviously, you have something to report. There's a sheriff in Garnet about fifty miles from Lodgepole."

He nodded but offered no further explanation. "Again, thank you." He let out a breath. "I'm Jude, by the way." His voice had a soft melodic quality.

"Lacey. I'm a biologist doing research on elk." She hoped he would return the favor and explain what he was doing up in these mountains.

He nodded but didn't say anything.

She maneuvered the truck through the heavy snow that had already piled up on the road. An object hit the truck with a violent thud. Her heart pounded as every muscle in her body tensed. The man with the rifle had thrown something at the truck.

"He must be out of bullets," said Jude. "I think he threw a rock at us."

Lacey glanced out of the driver's side window. The man was close enough for her to see his face. He ran toward them, rifle raised to be used as a blunt instrument. She saw him clearly. He was maybe ten feet away, a hulking mass of a man. The white-and-gray hair, the beard, the eyes that were filled with a murderous rage. A face she would not easily forget. The man looked right at her. A chill skittered over her skin.

She pressed the gas even harder, accelerating to a dangerous speed. She swerved.

Another blow struck the back end of the truck. In the rearview mirror, she saw the man raising his rifle to hit the truck again with the rifle stock.

Lacey gripped the steering wheel and chose the path of least resistance where the snow wasn't as deep. All the same, her truck drifted toward the edge of the road. She straightened her steering wheel, finally gaining control.

"Good job," said Jude. "That takes some skill." He still had a white-knuckle grip on the dashboard as he glanced nervously out the back window.

She had no idea what to think about this man sitting in her truck. He had a lot of explaining to do. She had never been a good judge of character. As her grandmother used to say, her people picker was broken. She did better with wilderness and animals.

"You handled the whole thing really well," said Jude.

"Thanks. So was that guy some sort of crazed landowner or something?" She really wanted to give Jude the benefit of the doubt, but she needed to know whom she had just rescued.

He took a moment to answer. He ran his fingers through his wavy brown hair. "No, it's a little more complicated than that. I'm a private investigator. That's all you need to know." He turned away and stared out the window.

Okay, so he wasn't going to tell her much. At least he was on the right side of the law.

When she checked the rearview mirror, she could no longer see the man with the rifle. But his face was burned into her memory. Though she could not say why. She had the feeling she had looked into the face of a murderer.

TWO

Lacey could see the tiny cluster of lights that was Lodgepole as she drove toward the base of the mountain. By the time she pulled onto Main Street, the wind and snow had intensified.

"Probably too dangerous to drive into Garnet to report what happened to you. Might have to wait until after the storm." She searched for a parking space.

"I suppose I can phone it in." His voice lacked commitment as he stared out the window. He seemed distracted. His mind must be on something else.

"If you can get a signal. Maybe we should do that together. I saw the guy pretty clearly."

Jude perked up. "Really?"

Downtown Lodgepole was all of five blocks long. Many of the businesses did double duty. She rolled past a post office that was also an information center for tourists. The hardware store advertised that you could get your car fixed there. There was one café next to the hotel where she was staying.

The Davenport Hotel had probably been the talk of the town when it was built at the turn of the century. Meant to be an elegant stopping place for weary railroad travelers, it was now run-down with only a few rooms still being used. Much of the hotel was boarded up and closed off. The railroad didn't come through Lodgepole anymore. No one came through here except the occasional hunter or hiker. She glanced over at Jude. And the occasional tight-lipped private investigator.

The residents of Lodgepole were not used to strangers and had a suspicion of them.

If she included the people who lived in remote cabins outside of Lodgepole, the population count might tick up by fifty. She'd been here for only a few days.

She pointed at the café. "We can find out about road conditions by going in there. The locals will give a better report than any weather channel or app on your phone. Are you hungry?"

"I really need to track that man down. I'll need to get another car. And I need you to describe him for me." A sense of urgency entered his voice. "I can't wait around here in this town."

"Sure, I can describe him. But honestly I don't think anybody is going anywhere." He seemed almost nervous now. Lunch might give him an opportunity for him to explain himself.

She headed toward the café which was also a sort of community center and place to get gossip and news. In addition to the cars parked on the street, there was probably an equal number of snowmobiles. Because the snow stayed almost year-round at this elevation and roads sometimes didn't get plowed quickly, snowmobiles were the preferred mode of transportation for most of the residents.

The second they pushed open the door and the tiny bell above it rang, the place fell silent. All eyes were on Jude and her. The chatter resumed almost immediately, but she felt the shift when she stepped into the café.

They weren't used to outsiders. She was still an outsider, and Jude wasn't from here either. Her research would keep her here for at least a month. People might warm up to her a little.

She searched the room for an empty table but didn't see one. All the seats at the counter were taken, as well. As she passed by the table, the talk was about the storm. She heard enough of the conversation to know the roads were already impassable.

She patted Jude's shoulder. "Looks like you're stuck here for a while."

The news didn't seem to sit well with Jude. His expression hardened.

A table opened up at the back of the café.

The teenage waitress came over and plopped down two menus. "We're out of the patty melt, but the tomato soup isn't too bad." The girl whirled away.

"Boy, she really sells that soup." Jude seemed to be mildly amused by the waitresses's casual behavior.

Lacey laughed and leaned forward, glad that he seemed to relax a little. "They probably just open up a can. It's not like the fresh produce truck makes its way up here." She liked the warmth she saw in his eyes and appreciated his effort at lightening his mood. "Maybe I could help you if you could tell me why that guy was after you."

Jude's forehead creased. He looked slightly off to the left. Then he leaned closer to her and spoke in a low voice. "A girl has been kidnapped. Part of the initial communication from the kidnapper was that the FBI not be contacted. But her father couldn't do nothing, so he hired me. Her father is a fairly well-known millionaire real estate developer in North Dakota. It's all got to be under the radar, or something bad might happen to the kid."

Lacey's breath caught in her throat as she absorbed the gravity of what he had just told her. Now she understood why he wasn't crazy about contacting the sheriff or being trapped in Lodgepole.

"It helps my case, but I'm concerned about you being able to identify him." He twirled the pepper shaker.

She spoke slowly. "You think he might follow us into town and try to hurt me?" Her old truck was distinct enough and Lodgepole was the only town for miles. It wouldn't be hard to figure out where they'd gone. Her heart squeezed tight.

"I don't know." Jude shook his head. "I just wish I wasn't stuck here. I was so close to catching him."

Lacey stared at the jelly packets and tried to process what Jude was implying. The man, who was probably a kidnapper, might come after her. "One good thing. If the roads are impassable for us, then he's stuck too. Either on that mountain or in town. Anyway, there are people around. I'm sure he wouldn't try anything." Her voice sounded weak, like she was trying to convince herself that she was safe.

* * *

Jude was grateful when the waitress walked back over to them before Lacey could ask him more questions. He'd already told her too much. He would be forever grateful to her for saving his life. She had been an answer to a very frantic prayer.

The waitress twirled a strand of her hair. "So, what will you two have?"

He hadn't had much time to study the menu. "A burger sounds great."

"I'll have the club sandwich." Lacey closed the menu and handed it over to the waitress.

He noticed the ketchup stain on his menu as he lifted it so the teenager could take it. This place had a certain uniqueness to it.

He turned his attention to Lacey. She kept her auburn hair tied up in a braid. Soft wisps of red hair framed her face. She offered him a brief smile when she caught him staring.

"You're not from around here?" he asked.

"I move around a lot for my research work." She rearranged the jam packets that were in the metal container.

"How about you tell me about your research."

Her eyes lit up and her whole face seemed to brighten. "I'm tracking the migrations and feeding patterns of an elk herd that mostly hang out on Shadow Ridge. I'm looking at how human activity might affect that." She continued to share details about her job. He liked the way she became so animated when she talked.

They continued to visit until most of the patrons had left the café. A silence fell between them.

Jude cleared his throat. "Are you okay with telling me what the man who shot at me looked like?" Though he didn't like making her revisit the attack, he needed to know if he was to find him.

Lacey stared at the table. "Yes, I can do that. Broad shoulders, built like a wrestler but older, gray-and-white hair, a beard. The expression on his face was…such rage." She shuddered.

He leaned toward her and patted her shoulder. "I still can't thank you enough for getting me out of there."

She nodded before glancing around the nearly empty café. "Looks like we closed the place down. I suppose we should get going. There is only one hotel in town."

When they stepped outside, it was pitch-dark. The wind had picked up, creating little tornadoes of snow swirling down the street. Jude buttoned his coat up against the cold. "I really want to have a look around this town.

If that guy did follow us down the mountain, he probably hid his car, but I could knock on a few doors with some kind of story. Maybe check some backyards. If there is only one hotel, I doubt he'd stay there."

"I don't think you would get very far in the dark and cold."

A gust of wind hit him. His eyes stung from the intensity of the cold. He could only see a few feet in front of him. His jaw clenched in frustration. "Okay maybe you're right. So, what is this hotel?"

"It's called the Davenport Hotel," she said.

"Guess I should stay there too." More than anything, he wanted to get back to tracking his suspect. Things were more complicated now that the suspect knew he'd been made and could be identified. He feared for the little girl's safety. If she was being held in one of the houses on that mountain road, would the man just leave her there to come into town after him and probably Lacey?

Several snowmobiles putted by, their headlights cutting through the blackness. Leaning into the wind, Lacey and Jude crossed the street and entered the hotel.

An old man slept in an overstuffed chair in the lobby. "That's Ray. He's the manager. Rather than wake him, I think we can just grab a key and leave him a note that you've got a room," she said. "You can pay him later or just leave the money in an envelope by the note. It's fifty dollars a night."

"Okay, if that is how it's done." The informality of the place only added to its charm. Jude pulled some money out of his wallet while Lacey found an envelope and paper to write on.

A wide sweeping staircase with an ornately carved bannister filled up most of the lobby. Though everything looked dusty, there was still a yesteryear elegance to the place. A huge mural of forest and wildlife, with a train puffing through it, took up one wall. Faded by time, it was nevertheless impressive. The trim on the ceiling looked like it had been carved by hand. The red carpet and matching velvet curtains indicated this had been quite the classy joint at one time.

Lacey walked behind the counter and grabbed a key. "You can have room ten right next to me. I'm in twelve. Some of the rooms aren't used anymore, but I know that one is."

They walked up the stairs together. Though frustration over being stranded made his jaw ache, meeting Lacey had been a nice reprieve. Lacey went back and forth between warmth and seeming guarded. Still, having dinner with her had been fun. *Fun* was not a word that was in his vocabulary much anymore… not for ten years.

She turned to face him. "Ray told me earlier today that two hunters checked in to the hotel this morning. Other than that, it's just us."

He touched a bannister, which was dusty. The whole place was probably not up to code. "They're probably glad to have your business."

"They gave me a deal since I'm going to be here a while doing research." She turned her key in the door. "Well, good night." She entered her room and closed the door behind her.

Jude sat down in his room. Though everything looked dated, it was very clean. He opened the bedside drawer and pulled his handgun out of the shoulder holster. He stared out the window as the snow fell with increasing volume and velocity. He didn't need to form any attachment to Lacey however temporary. He was here to find a kidnapped eight-year-old girl who was the daughter to millionaire George Ignatius.

Before becoming a private eye, Jude had been a police officer. He'd used his contacts in the department to get a trace of the vehicle that had abducted eight-year-old Maria. The home across the street from where she'd been kidnapped had a camera to record who came to the front door. Jude had isolated the time of the abduction on the recordings. The vehicle that took the little girl appeared in the background.

That trace on the vehicle had led him here. And now he couldn't do anything. From where he sat on the bed, he rested his elbows on his knees and his hands on the sides of his head. The rising frustration tied his stomach in knots.

This whole investigation might have gone sideways. His phone still wasn't getting a signal. If there was a landline, it probably wasn't working either. He couldn't call George. He'd never forgive himself if something happened to that little girl.

Again, he opened the drawer where he'd put his handgun. He hadn't noticed the Bible there before. Standard-issue even for this hotel. Not that he would ever open that book again. Not only did not being able to prevent the murder-suicide sideline his career, it stole his faith. He didn't know what he believed in anymore. That frantic prayer on the mountain when Lacey had shown up was the first time he'd prayed in ten years. And God had answered.

Jude lay down on top of the covers, staring at the copper ceiling, waiting for sleep to come.

He rubbed his chest where it felt tight. Though the kidnapper had not yet made a ransom demand, the clock was ticking for little Maria. A day ago the kidnapper had contacted George to let him know Maria was alive.

This storm moving in would delay his chance to search the residences that were on that mountain road. Even as the wind rattled the window, he could feel his chest tighten. He had to bring the girl home safe. In a way, he felt like his own life depended on that.

With the storm picking up intensity outside, Jude closed his eyes and willed himself to go to sleep. His last thought was of the auburn-haired Lacey. She was a hard woman to read, but she intrigued him. What was her story?

The heaviness of sleep invaded his muscles and he felt himself drifting off. He awoke to the sound of a woman screaming. Lacey was in trouble!

THREE

Lacey screamed when she awoke in total darkness, sensing that someone else was in her room. A footstep thudded in the darkness moving toward her.

Heart pounding, she fumbled for the bedside light. It didn't click on. The storm must have taken out the electricity. Her flashlight was in her backpack across the room. The curtains were pulled tight. She couldn't see anything. The darkness and being awakened from a deep sleep left her disoriented.

She could hear someone moving around the room.

"Who's there?" She cleared her throat, trying not to give away her fear in her voice. "What are you doing in my room?"

She swung around and let her feet fall on the carpet. What obstacles lay between her and that flashlight? She couldn't remember.

She took two steps before she hit a piece of furniture.

A body brushed up against her. Terror paralyzed her in her tracks. She could sense someone moving very close to her. Her heartbeat drummed in her ears.

Hands wrapped around her neck.

She twisted to one side before the attacker could grab hold of her.

Her heart beat so wildly, it felt like it would jump out of her chest. The man or woman reached out and tugged at her shirt, probably trying to grab her again or feel their way in the darkness. She whirled away, crashing into more furniture.

Someone pounded on the door. "Lacey, is everything okay in there?"

It was Jude.

She opened her mouth to speak but no words came out. Terror had stolen her voice.

She could hear the intruder fumbling around. Jude was shaking the doorknob.

"Lacey, come on, open up."

She stumbled across the dark room, feeling along the wall until she found the doorknob. She unfastened the dead bolt and swung open the door.

Jude shone a flashlight into the room. "What's going on?"

The light bounced around the room. Lacey got only a glimpse of her intruder before he exited out of the other door on the other side of the room. All she could say for sure was that he was a tall thin man. Not the broad-shouldered man she'd seen on the mountain.

Lacey grabbed Jude's flashlight and ran in the direction the man had gone. The door where the intruder had escaped was ajar. The place was so low security it had been un-locked. She entered an adjoining room that was not occupied but must have been part of a suite that connected to her room at one time. She shone the flashlight all around. The man was gone.

Jude came up behind her. "What's going on and can I have my flashlight back?"

"Sorry." She handed it back to him. "There was somebody in my room."

"I'll see if I can catch him." Jude's foot-steps pounded up the hallway and then faded.

She was left in the dark. A rush of terror over the assault, which may have been an at-tempt on her life, caused her knees to turn to mush.

Jude returned. "I couldn't see anyone. I don't know the layout of this place. There are a bunch of boarded up areas. I searched as best I could. I think he must have escaped."

"I'm sure there is more than one door he could have slipped out of." Her voice still vibrated with fear.

Jude's words filled with compassion. "I would have gotten to you faster from my room. It took a minute to find my flashlight in the dark. Why don't you come back and sit down?" He led her gently back into the room and pointed her toward a chair. He stood at the window and pulled back the curtain. "Looks like the power is out all over town."

She stared out the window. Her room faced the back of the hotel, so they were looking at residences. All the windows in the houses were dark. She saw only the occasional tiny glow of light coming from a flashlight or a lantern or maybe even a candle.

She wrapped her arms around herself, still trying to process what had just happened.

Jude patted her hand before sitting in the chair opposite her. "Did you get a look at him? Was it the man who came after me?"

She shook her head. "I didn't see his face. But he was the wrong build for the man we saw on the mountain."

"Hate to say it, but sometimes people take advantage of blackouts and decide to rob people," Jude said.

"I suppose I would be a prime target since

I'm not from around here." She touched her neck, remembering that the man had tried to grab her or maybe he'd just been fumbling in the dark. But she was not able to shake off the fear that had sunk into her bones that the attack was connected to what had happened on that mountain road. "Or the man who came after you has an accomplice." She couldn't stop shaking.

Jude touched her shoulder. "Hey, it's all right now. You're safe."

She appreciated his kindness, but her heart was still racing.

Footsteps pounded on the stairs and Ray, the old man from the lobby, appeared in their open doorway holding a camping lantern. He held it close to his cheek, so half his face was in shadow and the other half was lit up. "You two are awake. Heard a ruckus up here." He looked at Jude. "You the fella that left a note?"

Jude nodded. "Yes."

"What's all the noise about?" Ray leaned forward to peer in the room.

"Someone was in Lacey's room," said Jude. "Did you see anyone?"

"No," said Ray. "Only two other people are staying at the hotel."

Ray stood still, holding the lantern, studying both their faces while his was still half-covered in shadow. Did he think they were making this up?

"All I know is someone attacked Lacey," said Jude.

Ray took a step back. "Electricity is out all over town. Got a fire started in the ballroom and some snacks," said Ray. Without waiting for their response, he disappeared down the hallway. The old man either didn't believe him or didn't want to deal with another problem right now.

The wind rattled the windows. Lacey got to her feet. "We might as well go downstairs. I'm not going to fall back asleep."

The signs indicated that the ballroom was in the west end of the hotel. The room was huge with wooden floors. Two chandeliers hung from the ceiling. Lacey could picture the parties, dances and banquets that must have taken place here.

Now it was completely empty except for a table, couch and comfy-looking chairs that surrounded the crackling fire. The air smelled like wood polish. Another lantern had been set up on the table. Store-bought cookies, cold cuts, cheese and crackers had been set out. There was also a camp stove with a teakettle on it. All the fixings for cocoa and tea sat beside the stove.

A moment later, two men entered the ballroom and found a seat. Lacey's heart fluttered. Both the men were the same build as the man who had attacked her. Come to think of it, so was Ray.

The older man pointed to the younger. "I'm Eddie and this is my son Jonathan. Looks like we are in for a long night."

Lacey and Jude introduced themselves.

Lacey grabbed a paper plate and some food. When she sat down in a high-back chair, the heat from the fire calmed her. The men made small talk while Lacey stared at the fire.

Ray entered the ballroom. "Things have gotten even worse in the last twenty minutes. It's whiteout conditions outside. A man could walk only a few feet, get disoriented and freeze to death," said Ray. "Until this storm subsides, you cannot go outside. You'd be taking your life in your own hands."

Lacey's throat constricted. "So if someone was in the hotel, they couldn't leave, right?"

"Not unless they wanted to risk death," said Ray. "Nope, the smart thing to do is to stay put until this thing dies down."

The cookie Lacey was nibbling didn't taste

so sweet anymore. She stared at all the men. The only one who was off the hook for attacking her was Jude. He'd come to the door and spoken while the other man was running away.

It was possible too that the three men were innocent and the attacker was hiding somewhere in the hotel. Both alternatives sent a wave of terror through her.

As he snacked on his cheese and crackers, Jude noticed a shift in mood for Lacey. She stared at the fire and gave one-word answers when anyone tried to include her in the conversation. She rubbed her feet together as though nervous.

He felt a little restless himself. How was eight-year-old Maria doing? Was she safe? Was she alone and hungry? His only comfort was that if he was trapped, maybe the kidnapper was too. Once the storm broke, he might still be able to search the houses that connected with that road. Maybe Maria had even been in the car when Jude had been shot at. The kidnapper could have brought her down here and was hiding her somewhere. There were too many unknowns. All he knew was that the longer he was delayed, the colder this case got and the less of a chance that Maria would be returned alive.

Maybe Lacey was right. Maybe the kidnapper had an accomplice. Lacey could identify him, but Jude was the one who had been on his tail. Jude figured it was only a matter of time before he became a target too.

When there was a lull in the conversation, Lacey bolted up from her chair. "You know, I think I'll go upstairs. Are you coming, Jude? I need to talk to you about something."

"Sure." What was she up to?

Jude nodded his goodbye to the other men and then walked with Lacey across the expansive wood floor.

Once they were out of earshot in the hallway, Lacey turned toward him. Desperation filled her voice. "Help me search the hotel."

"What are you talking about?"

"Ray said there was no way anyone would go out in this. Whoever attacked me must still be hiding in this hotel. He must have snuck in before the storm got so bad," she said. "I want to know what he was doing in my room. And I want to know that it won't happen again because he's been caught."

He heard the fear in her voice. "Sure. It's not like I have a busy social schedule." He hoped the attack on Lacey wasn't connected to the kidnapping. It was a thin hope at best. He didn't like the idea of Lacey being in danger after she had risked her life to save his.

"Okay, come with me so I can get my flashlight out of my room," she said.

She headed toward the stairs, moving outside of the cone of illumination his flashlight made.

"I don't want the others to know we're looking. Just in case it was one of them who was in my room." She stepped on the first stair and turned, waiting for him to come toward her with the light.

They hurried upstairs. While Lacey got her flashlight, Jude retrieved his gun from the nightstand drawer. He shoved it in his waistband at the back and untucked his flannel shirt so it would be covered.

Had Lacey been chosen at random to be robbed? Had she been chosen because as a woman she was more vulnerable? Or was this connected to what had happened on the mountain?

They met in the hallway, both of them holding flashlights. "Let's search this floor first," she said. "He ran off this way. At the time, I just assumed he took a back entrance and escaped out into the night."

He spoke in a low voice as they made their

way down the hallway. "Is there something controversial about your research?"

She swung the flashlight back and forth after stepping into an area that may have been some sort of meeting place for hotel guests. There was a fireplace in the center of the room and a very dusty-looking oriental rug. A couple of cardboard boxes were stacked in a corner.

"I don't think there is anything controversial about my research. If anything, it helps hunters and campers. Why are you asking?"

"Just trying to figure out a motive for the attack." He really wanted the attack to be unconnected to the kidnapping.

"Motive for the attack? You sound like a cop." She shone her flashlight in his direction.

"I used to be." The comment was friendly enough, but he could feel himself retreat emotionally. "Let's just leave it at that."

"Sure, Jude." She swept past him and up the hall, then looked over her shoulder. Even in near darkness her auburn hair had a glossy sheen to it. "I told you everything about my job, but you don't want to talk about yours."

He hurried after her. "I said I used to be a cop."

"So why did you stop being a cop?" She stood in front of an ancient-looking elevator with an out-of-order sign. Her gaze rested on him, waiting for a response.

He reached out and touched the out-of-order sign that looked like it might have been hung during the Carter administration. "Let's take the stairs." Jude felt like someone had stirred his insides with a hot poker. Thinking about the past did that to him.

He'd kept all the pain from his past at bay, but here was this redheaded woman showing curiosity about who he was as a man. A part of him wanted to open up to her just to have another person bear the burden with him.

Lacey bounded down two flights of stairs. "He probably wouldn't hide on the main floor since it is the most used." At the bottom of the stairs was a large wooden door.

Jude pushed on it. It screeched open, revealing a dark corridor with a series of doors and walls made of stone.

Lacey held the flashlight up to her chin and spoke theatrically. "The belly of the whale."

He laughed. Her sense of humor was infectious. "You go first, my lady. I'll back you up." Maybe too, the humor covered up the fear she must be wrestling with.

They brushed away cobwebs and stepped into the hallway. Their footsteps echoed on the concrete. Each room they searched revealed various items: stored furniture, a broken chandelier and some kitchen appliances. All of it looked like it hadn't been used in a long time. Lacey stepped into the room where a stove was stored. She shone a light on the dusty surface. Her body went rigid.

Jude stepped toward her. "What is it?"

"This looks fresh to me." She aimed her light on the dusty stove top where there was a handprint.

Jude shone his light all around the concrete room. All the other rooms had had an abundance of cobwebs but not this one. "Yeah maybe someone was in here recently."

He saw the fear in her eyes. He patted her shoulder, hoping to comfort her. They continued their search. "It could have been Ray for whatever reason."

The only room that looked like it was used on a regular basis was the laundry room, which was clean and contained folded linens, three washing machines and two dryers. Some towels hung over a drying rack. They had worked their way down the entire corridor to the other end of the hotel where there was another staircase leading back to the main floor.

"Let's head back upstairs," he said.

She rubbed her forehead, still standing at

the base of the stairs. "The one thing I know for sure is that someone was in my room and that at one point they had their hands around my neck." Her voice faltered.

He leaned a little closer to her. "I know an attack like that can be really scary. I think the best thing to do would be to try to get some sleep. If it would help at all, I can sleep in the chair in your room."

"Thank you. I think I need that." She turned to face him. "We were strangers less than ten hours ago. I guess we're in this together for now."

He did feel a bond growing between them. It was unusual for him to have an instant connection with anyone. His relationships with women seemed to fall apart before they ever got started. There wasn't much he could do about liking Lacey other than enjoy the time they did have together. His work here would be finished soon enough, hopefully with a happy ending. He'd head back to North Dakota. His gut twisted into a tight knot when he thought about the kidnapped child.

They made their way upstairs, taking a little time to search the main floor. Laughter spilled out from the ballroom. When they peeked inside Ray and Eddie had set up a chessboard. Eddie's son must have returned to his room.

They stepped away from the ballroom and headed back to their rooms. They stood on the mezzanine looking down on the ornate but worn carpet in the lobby.

The most likely scenario was that whoever had been in Lacey's room had been there to rob her. All the same, he could not shut off his cop mind. "Is there some reason why someone in this town might be mad at you or your family?"

"I don't have any connection to this town. I'm from the other side of the state." She leaned forward, gripping the railing with her hands and staring off into space.

"I thought you said that you moved around a lot?"

"I do. I live in forest service cabins and campers mostly. I grew up in a little town called Jasper." Her voice faltered. "Haven't been back there in years."

There was a depth of emotion to her comment that he could not begin to plumb. He suspected that there was a tragic amount of pain to her statement. "What about your mom and your dad?"

"They're dead along with my little brother. The only family I have is my grandmother.

Honestly, I don't think my family has anything to do with why I was attacked."

Jude felt as though all the air had left the room. He picked up on her defensive tone. "I wasn't prying. I'm just trying to figure this thing out."

Lacey turned toward him. "Sorry, it's a time waster to ask questions about my family, okay?"

Just like him she'd grown defensive when talking about the past.

Jude cleared his throat. He stepped away from the bannister. "Why don't we try to get some sleep. If he is still here in the hotel, I'll keep watch for him."

She studied him for a long moment. "Okay…thank you." She walked the few feet to her room and shut the door behind her. Jude returned to his room to grab his phone, which had a book on it he'd been reading. He knocked on her door. Lacey opened it.

He collapsed into the chair. She got into bed and rolled over.

Jude read for about twenty minutes, dozed and woke up. He'd left the flashlight on to provide some light. A small tattered Bible sat on her nightstand. Maybe her tragic loss had deepened her faith instead of stolen it. It seemed though that both of them had been running each in a different way. Her job meant she didn't put down roots or connect to a community. After the shooting, he'd quit the force and closed himself off, preferring to put his energy into his work. Lacey was the first person he'd felt any connection to in ten years.

He couldn't begin to sort through the emotional rupture that had risen up between them. Right now, he needed to focus on keeping Lacey safe. The storm continued to rage outside as Jude struggled to calm his restless mind.

FOUR

Lacey awoke. She turned sideways. Jude was no longer in his chair. Even though he might have just slipped out to get something in his room, she felt less safe when he wasn't close. His agreeing to sit watch was the only reason she'd slept at all. Early morning light shone in from the window. The storm had let up, improving visibility, but it was still snowing.

She heard a noise outside her door.

Her heart beat a little faster. "Jude, is that you?" She ran to the door and flung it open expecting to see him. There was no one on the mezzanine. Now she realized that maybe the noise had come from downstairs. She stepped toward the banister. Down below, she watched as a tall thin figure hurried through the lobby and slipped outside. He'd been wearing a hat, so she couldn't see what color his hair was.

That had to be her attacker.

She stood on the mezzanine as she reached out for the wall for support.

Lacey's heart thumped in her chest. The man had taken advantage of the letup in the storm to escape. Fear permeated her whole being.

A heavy silence enveloped her as she fought the terror that raged through her. Seeing the man brought back the trauma of the attack.

Jude came up the hallway and she fell into his arms.

"Hey, Lacey, what happened?"

"I saw him. He left the hotel. He was here all night." Her voice must have given away how upset she was.

"Hey." Jude gave her a tight reassuring hug and then stepped back to look at her. Jude led her over to the plush velvet chairs that were outside the hotel room on the mezzanine. "Sit down and catch your breath. How long ago? Maybe I can catch him."

"It's been a few minutes. I'm sure he's gone by now." She placed her hand on her heart and took in a deep breath. "Where did you go, anyway? I woke up and you weren't there."

"I just went down the hall to use the facilities." The hotel was so old that there was only one bathroom per floor. He rested his hand on her shoulder. "I'm sorry."

His hand lingered on her shoulder, and the warmth of his touch soaked through the fabric of her shirt. She'd always thought of herself as a free spirit, someone who didn't need anyone. But given what had happened to her, she kind of liked having Jude around. Just his presence seemed to smooth over the agitation and fear.

"If he is connected to the kidnapper, why hasn't he come after me?"

She turned to face him. "There you go again being a detective."

"I'm trying to figure this thing out." Jude shifted in his chair.

She crossed her arms over her chest. "Maybe I'm just the easier target." She slumped back in the chair. "I do know one thing. I don't like feeling like I'm trapped in this hotel." But going outside meant the tall thin man might come after her.

Ray walked into the lobby holding a box. He shouted up at them. "Storm won't be the worst of it. It's the aftermath. Be a few days before the plows dig us out and the roads are passable." Ray must have heard what she'd said.

Jude let out a heavy breath.

Ray rested the box on the counter and pulled out a package. "Got some beef jerky here if you folks are hungry."

Jude rose, leaned over the railing and held up his hands. Ray tossed him a package. "Fine dining at its best."

Ray pointed to the box. "There's more food in here if you want to top off the meal with some granola bars. Bottled water is in the kitchen." Ray pointed to a door on the other side of the checkout counter. "Eddie and son have already helped themselves."

"So they are both still here?" said Lacey.

Ray drew his head back, so his chin touched his neck and a look of confusion crossed his features. "Sure, why wouldn't they be?"

Lacey shrugged.

Ray walked over to the window and placed his hands on his hips. "Four or five more hours. This should clear up enough to walk around town at least." He turned back to face them, rubbing his chin. "Still won't be any electricity."

Ray, the bringer of bad news, ambled away.

Jude rose to his feet and held out a hand for Lacey. "Might as well make the best of it."

She took his hand, feeling the strength of his grip and the calluses on his palms. She met his gaze for just a moment, his soft eyes resting on her.

After finding food and water in the kitchen, Jude and Lacey returned to the ballroom to wait the storm out by playing a game of chess. They played two games.

"That's it. You beat me," Jude said.

"So we're even. You beat me last time. Want to go for a third game to see if we can determine who the true champion is?"

Jude yawned. "You know I think I might just close my eyes for a minute. I didn't sleep much last night."

"Okay." Of course, he was tired. He'd stayed up half the night watching over her.

She got up and wandered the ballroom toward a far wall where other books and games were stored on shelves. She pulled a book from the shelf that looked like it might hold her attention and then sat down in the easy chair opposite Jude, who was already snoring. He looked kind of cute sleeping with his mouth open. His wavy hair flopped over his forehead.

She'd never spent this much time with another person. Other than her little brother when he was alive. Pain shot through her as though a sword had been driven through her chest. So much had been ripped from her life. She knew that there was a part of her that just didn't dare open her heart again to ever caring about another person.

She liked being with Jude. He was funny

and easy to be with. But theirs was a tempo-rary and fragile arrangement. All she needed was God, her job and her beat-up truck.

She thanked God for the brief reprieve she'd gotten from his company.

She read for a while, threw another log on the fire and then dozed herself. Her nap was interrupted by Ray towering over her.

"Put your snow gear on if you like. People are starting to dig out and emerge. Most peo-ple are congregating over at the school on the other side of town, up a few blocks. They have a generator and food. Any announcement that town folk need to hear will be made there."

Jude had stirred awake, as well. It took them only minutes to race upstairs and get into their boots and coats. They both emerged from their rooms laughing.

"I didn't realize how bad my cabin fever was until now," he said.

Lacey and Jude bounded down the stairs and out into the open. Her elation changed to fear. The tall thin man was out here some-where.

The snow had drifted in front of some of the doors of the shops and in the street, as well. Some snow still twirled out of the overcast sky. But she could see structures and people.

He tugged on her coat. "I have no idea

where the school is. First let's take a look around and see if we can spot the man you saw at the hotel. If that other guy did come down off the mountain, I doubt he'd be out in the open, but he's my lead for finding Maria. I have to search for him and his car."

Lacey tensed as a wave of fear rolled over her. "I didn't get a good look at the tall thin man."

"I'll stay with you, promise." He squeezed her arm just above the elbow and then winked at her, which made her smile. "I have to do my job even with this storm."

It looked like she and Jude were going to continue to be together for safety if nothing else.

In her brief survey of the town as she'd driven toward the hotel when she'd first arrived, she didn't remember seeing any buildings that looked like a school. She tilted her head toward the sky and let the flakes melt on her cheeks.

"Ray said the school is not on Main Street. I'm sure we can ask someone to get more specific directions if we can't find it, but let's have a look around."

"Just describe the man you saw and say you're looking for him. No one needs to know about Maria," Jude said.

He stopped to ask several people who were

outside their homes clearing away snow if they had seen the car or the man from the mountain. He offered a description. None of them had.

Lacey stared down the street. "What if we split up. I can go this way up the street."

"Okay, but stay on this street so you're in my sight," Jude said.

Lacey worked her way up the street knocking on several doors. One was occupied by an old woman and another by a woman with kids hanging on her skirt. None of them had seen the man she described or the car. When she peered around the side of the houses she didn't see a car that resembled the one that had run Jude off the road. The Davenport was the only hotel in town. If the man was in town, he must be hiding out in a house or maybe there was an abandoned building somewhere.

She walked past an empty lot where a house may have been at one time. When she glanced up the sidewalk, Jude was knocking on another door. The final house she came to was a weathered-looking blue Victorian. She ran up the creaking steps and knocked, waited and knocked again. She stepped down the stairs and peered into the big front windows. It didn't look like anyone was home.

Movement on the upper floor window caught her attention. A man with jet-black hair and a beefy build stared down at her. He locked her in his gaze and then slipped back into the shadows.

Her skin tingled. Why hadn't he answered the door?

Jude was coming up the walk toward her. She ran to meet him, brushing off the rudeness of the man at the upper window. Some people were just antisocial. She met Jude in the middle of the block.

"There's some more houses over there we can check out," Jude said, pointing at a group of houses that lay just beyond an open field.

She followed him with a backward glance toward the blue Victorian house. They wandered toward a side street and then into an open field that was probably for baseball or soccer. The field was set apart from the rest of the town, but there were houses on the other side of it some distance away.

All around them she could hear the sounds of the town coming to life. She heard children laughing in the distance and snowmobiles motoring around.

They were midway across the wide field when the sound of a snowmobile caught her attention. She looked up to see a snowmobile headed straight toward them.

It took a second for it to register in Jude's brain that the driver of the snowmobile intended to plow them down. He grabbed Lacey and pushed her toward a snowdrift, landing beside her as the vehicle whizzed past them. The driver had on a helmet with a dark visor.

Heart racing, he pulled Lacey to her feet.

Again, the roar of an engine surrounded them. The driver had turned around and was making a second pass at them, barreling toward them at a high rate of speed. Both of them crawled over the drift and ran toward a grove of trees.

The clang and rumble of the snowmobile engine engulfed them as they sprinted toward the safety of the trees. The grove wasn't that big, maybe fifty feet across. The snowmobiler circled around it as though taunting them that they could not escape.

Out of breath, Lacey touched her gloved hand to her chest. "What in the world?"

He gathered her into his arms and held her close. Partly to quell her fear but also because having her close made him feel less afraid.

The snowmobile did another circle around

them. The noise of the engine was menacing and oppressive.

"Either people in this town really don't like outsiders, or someone is after us." Her voice trembled.

He held her close even as the noise of the snowmobile echoed through the trees. The guy wasn't just going to give up and leave.

He glanced through the bare trees at the snowmobile. "When he gets to the back side of these trees—" Jude pointed out across the field where the houses on the edge of town were visible "—I say we make a run for it."

"I don't know if I can."

When he looked into her eyes, he saw the fear there, how shaken she was by all this. Jude touched her cheek with his gloved hand. "You can do this. Those houses are not that far away. I doubt he'll come after us in broad daylight with people around."

"It's got to be the same guy who was at the hotel. Don't you think?"

"Probably. Let's just get to where it's safe." He watched the snowmobile circle around behind the trees. "Now, Lacey, now." He grabbed her hand and pulled her through the trees.

Their boots pressed into the deep and drifted snow slowing them in their flight.

Behind him, Jude could hear the snowmobile growing louder.

He hoped he had not made a mistake and put Lacey in even greater danger. He could see the backyards of the houses up ahead. But no people.

Gripping Lacey's hand, he sprinted even faster. She kept pace with him. The mumbling roar of the snowmobile pressed on his ears drawing ever closer.

Then suddenly it stopped altogether.

Jude glanced over his shoulder. The snowmobiler had parked, still perched on the machine with the engine running. Then Jude drew his attention to the scene in front of him. They were still about fifty yards from the backyards of the houses. A man had come around with a snowblower and was trying to clear a path while his children played behind him.

The snowmobiler revved his engine and was turning away, disappearing on the other side of the trees, so the guy didn't want any witnesses.

Out of breath, Lacey and Jude slowed their pace, reaching the houses on the edge of town. The snowblower was too loud and the man too focused to get his attention. Jude and Lacey approached the three children.

Two were lying in the snow making snow angels while the third caught snowflakes on her tongue.

Jude's heart was still racing as he walked toward the girl catching snowflakes. "Did you guys see that guy on the snowmobile?"

The girl, who was maybe seven, wiped moisture off her forehead. "Yeah."

"I don't suppose you know who owns that snowmobile." Jude leaned so he was closer to the girl.

The girl studied him with dark pensive eyes. "Everybody has one. They kind of all look alike."

It had been a long shot. There was nothing distinct about the snowmobile, no paint job or custom design that would make it stand out. The driver as well had been in a brown snowsuit and black helmet.

"Can you point us toward the school?" Lacey stood beside Jude, their shoulders touching.

One of the snow-angel makers, a boy, sat up, "That's where everyone is going. We're headed up there as soon as Dad makes a path." The boy pointed to the man with the snowblower.

The girl pointed up the street. "You go back to the street where the restaurant is and then turn and walk up."

"Thanks." Jude trudged up the sidewalk

which was still filled with snow. Lacey walked beside him. "Why are we going to the school?"

"I'm thinking it would be safer with people around," Jude said. "Maybe I can borrow a snowmobile to get out of town and search that mountain."

"You're probably right." She looped her arm through his. Maybe it was just because she'd had such a fright that she wanted to be close to him. All the same, he liked that she trusted him that much.

The houses were still mostly dark. He saw only a faint light here and there in windows from a candle or lantern. An overcast sky veiled the full intensity of the sun. It felt a little like they were under a dome.

They found their way back to Main Street where there were more signs of activity, more people digging out. Still no cars moved up and down the street. Some men shoveled around where their snowmobiles were buried beneath several feet of snow. The café where they had met was dark as they walked past it.

They trudged about two blocks before what was clearly the school came into view. A front school yard filled with very dated play equipment made of metal and a brick building with another smaller stick-built house next to it. He suspected that at one time the house had been where the schoolteacher lived though it might not be used for that now.

Light glowed from every window and there was a steady stream of people coming from different parts of town headed toward the wide concrete steps.

Lacey jerked.

"Are you okay with this?"

"I'm not sure what choice we have." She tilted her head to look into his eyes.

She looked kind of cute with the snow falling all around her, her beanie hat, red hair framing her porcelain face.

"That guy on the snowmobile, whomever he is, doesn't want witnesses. We should be pretty safe staying here," he reasoned. He wanted to search more, but he knew he couldn't leave Lacey alone.

"Well, one thing is for sure. I'll go crazy if I have to hang out in that hotel," she said.

He laughed. Both of them could agree on that. They headed toward the steps. Jude nodded at the other people going inside. Plenty of them were tall and thin. He wondered if any of them had come after Lacey and him intent on harm less than twenty minutes ago.

Or was the culprit hiding out somewhere in some dark home, waiting for another chance to strike?

FIVE

A tension twisted through Lacey's chest, making it hard to breathe. Yes, there was a good chance whoever had entered her hotel room and then tried to mow Jude and her down with a snowmobile was among the people going into the school. And there was a chance he was the kidnapper's accomplice.

They stepped into a sort of lobby area where there were cubbies and places for kids to hang up their coats. There were two doors on either side of them and a wide hallway in the middle with two large doors at the end. A woman in a sweater that had light-up reindeer on it stepped toward them. Her graying blond hair was piled on her head in a series of twists and braids.

"You two look lost," the woman said, stepping toward them. "This must be your first Lodgepole snowstorm."

"Yes," Jude said. "I guess we kind of stick out from everyone else."

The woman had a warm smile. "Not to worry. Most people in the classrooms are just socializing. We have coffee and tea set up. The rest of us are in the gym trying to put some hot food together to feed everyone."

Lacey tugged on Jude's sleeve. "We'll come give you a hand with the meal." That way they could stay together. Lacey had worked in enough small towns to know that the way to win people over was to pitch in with whatever work was at hand. Plus, if Jude wanted to borrow a snowmobile, he'd have to win the trust of the townspeople first.

The woman's face lit up. "Oh delightful. We can use all the help we can get. I'm Terri by the way," the woman said.

"I'm Jude and this is Lacey."

"Follow me." Terri spoke over her shoulder as she walked down the wide hallway. "Don't tell me you two came here on your honeymoon to cash in on the winter activities."

"Actually, we didn't know each other until a day ago," Jude said.

Jude shot Lacey a look, raising his eyebrows. She shrugged. So, they had given Terri the impression that they were a couple.

Terri pushed open one of the wide doors.

They stepped into what was a sort of all-purpose room for the little school. There was a gym floor marked off for half-court basketball and a stage at one end. A piano sat in a corner.

Terri pointed to a door off to the side. "The kitchen is in there. There's plenty of chopping and mixing to do." She looked at Jude. "And in a little bit we'll need to set up some tables and chairs."

They entered the kitchen where several older women and two teenagers, a boy and a girl, were at work. The boy, who was loading a dishwasher, was too chubby to have been her attacker.

"We're here to help," Lacey said to the elderly woman who appeared to be in charge.

The woman smiled and pointed over to where the girl was chopping vegetables. "We're hoping to get some kind of meal for a crowd thrown together." She eyed Jude. "You look like you would be good at cutting up chicken."

Lacey set to work with the teenage girl chopping vegetables while Jude aided in dicing chicken. From the talk of the other women, the plan was to make some pots of chicken soup and some salads. The women were warm and welcoming. The older women had stories to tell about previous snowstorms.

They asked Lacey questions about her work. Quite a switch from the earlier reception when she'd first come into town. Maybe it just took a while for people in Lodgepole to warm up to strangers. Nothing like a snow-storm to draw out the best in people.

She noticed that Jude still wasn't volunteering much information. He must be tight-lipped with everyone.

As the ladies joked and laughed, she caught herself stealing looks at Jude who seemed to be enjoying the company, as well. He met her gaze for just a moment. Other people, strangers, had looked at them and thought they were involved. Her heart fluttered a little when he caught her in his gaze. Maybe there was an attraction there.

One of the older women tapped Jude on the shoulder. "You look big and strong. If you go down in the basement, there's a pantry. I'm going to need one of those bags of flour to make my biscuits. I can't carry such a heavy thing up the stairs."

Jude glanced in Lacey's direction. Whatever the reasons for the attacks, these people were not dangerous. She could stay in the safety of the kitchen until Jude got back. "Sure, no problem."

Another woman caught Jude on his way

out and handed him a piece of paper. "Before you go. I wrote down some other things we'll need from the basement."

Jude took the note and headed out the door.

Once Jude was gone, one of the older women sidled up to Lacey and knocked her shoulder against Lacey's. "Hubba-hubba."

"What?"

The older woman tilted her head to where Jude had just gone. "If I was a little younger. How wonderful for you. He's handsome and he likes to help out in the kitchen."

Heat rose up in Lacey's cheeks. "No, we're not…" Oh, what was the use? These women were convinced she and Jude were together. Maybe they were seeing something she wasn't willing to admit. She and Jude had been thrown together because they were outsiders and now she appreciated the protection he offered until they weren't stranded in this town and they could let law enforcement know about the attacks. But Jude was just as guarded as she was. Once the roads opened up, she suspected they would part ways.

Jude returned a few minutes later with the flour and the promise that he would bring the other stuff up. He disappeared again. While the pots of soup boiled, Lacey helped chopped vegetables for a salad. At least ten minutes passed with no sign of Jude. She grew worried that something bad had happened to him.

She excused herself and searched for the door the women indicated led to the food storage area. She headed down the stairs. There were rows and rows of shelves stocked with all sorts of canned goods as well as some in plastic tubs with labels on them like flour and sugar. Another shelf had first aid kits, water and thermal blankets. The town was clearly prepared for disasters like a snowstorm.

"Jude?"

It looked like there was a hallway on the other side of the storage room.

"Jude? Are you down here?" Above her, she could hear people stomping around and laughing. There was a scraping sound like tables and chairs being set up. She heard footsteps on the stairs she had just come down. She couldn't see around the shelves. The footsteps came toward her. Fear encroached.

A young pregnant woman came around the first wall of metal shelves. "Oh, I didn't know someone else was down here," the pregnant woman said. "I was just looking for some napkins. We should be eating here pretty soon."

"I think I saw some a couple shelves over." Lacey helped the woman find the napkins. She listened to her footsteps tap up the stairs.

Convinced that Jude must have gone somewhere else, she was about ready to head back up the stairs herself when she heard a screeching noise deeper in the basement.

She stepped out into a hallway where she'd heard the sound. "Jude?"

Someone grabbed her from behind, cupping a hand over her mouth and dragging her down the hallway. She struggled to break free or at least scream for help. The man held her in his tight grip, dragging her farther down the hall.

She kicked and tried to twist free.

He let go of her. She felt herself being pushed. A door slammed. Cold enveloped her. She was inside a walk-in freezer. A single lightbulb hung from the ceiling. She banged on the door and shouted for a full five minutes. Her fists hurt from pounding.

Already the chill had sunk into her skin. She could feel her body shutting down. Her mind fogged.

Above her, she could hear people moving around. Settling in to eat a meal together. The cooking was done. It was unlikely anyone would come back down the stairs for at least twenty minutes. By then she would freeze to death.

Jude stared around at the throngs of people as they shuffled into the gym. Some stood in line to get their food. Others were already sitting down enjoying their soup. He didn't see Lacey anywhere.

He'd gotten tangled in a conversation he couldn't get out of for just a few minutes.

He popped his head in the kitchen. Only two of the women remained. "Have you seen Lacey?"

Both of them shook their heads.

"She might have gone looking for you," one of the women said.

Jude hurried down the stairs to where the food and supplies were stored. He called Lacey's name. He raced around the tall shelves.

A pounding noise led him down a hallway to a walk-in freezer. He swung the door open and Lacey fell into his arms. She was crying and shivering.

"Stay here, you're going to be okay." He ran back to the supply shelves and grabbed one of the thermal blankets. He enveloped her with it. She tucked in close to him as he led her up the hallway.

She backed up against the wall and slid down to the floor. He pulled the blanket over her shoulders and sat next to her.

"Someone pushed you in there?"

She nodded, still unable to speak.

He wrapped his arms around her and held her close. After a while, she stopped shivering.

"This has to be connected to what happened on the mountain. The people in this town might not like outsiders but they're not killers." She turned her face toward him and wept.

She swiped at her eyes.

He continued to hold her as her tears dampened his neck. He rested his hand on her shoulder. "I don't know what is going on here, Lacey. But you are safe now. I'm here." And it was clear he needed to stay close to her no matter what, for her protection.

She pulled away so she could make eye contact, her gaze searching. "I thought I was going to die in there."

"But you didn't." He looked into her eyes.

"That thing about your whole life flashing before your eyes is true." She drew the blanket around herself. "I mean, it's not like I saw everything that happened to me. But I could feel my body and my brain slowing down. And I just wondered if the life I'd lived mattered. To other people, to God especially."

He pulled away. "God and I are kind of not on speaking terms."

"But you were at one time?"

Jude took in a deep breath. He had to tell her the truth. "It's a long story. Two people died on my watch back when I was on the force. I prayed I would be able to prevent it." He shook his head as the bitter taste over what had happened, over what he could not stop, rose up inside of him. "There was a child who witnessed the murder-suicide. She will never be the same."

"After my parents and my brother died, I just figured I could get through with just me and God." She tilted her head toward the ceiling where they could hear the sound of people enjoying food and fellowship. She shrugged. "Now I don't know. Maybe that was wrong thinking. I really thought I was going to freeze to death in there."

The experience had made them both want to share more about themselves.

He hugged her and held her close. "I'm glad you didn't." He hesitated but then plunged forward even as fear wanted to steal his words from him. "This last day or so with you, Lacey. It's been nice…in an unexpected way."

She elbowed him playfully. "Thanks. You've been a good surprise too."

Jude stared at the ceiling, tightening his arms around Lacey. Her soft hair brushed his cheek. While he relished this moment they had together, it was clear that wherever they went in this town they were not safe.

SIX

Lacey turned to face Jude, staring into his brown eyes. His expression had grown serious as he pulled away from her. He stared at the floor and then rose to his feet.

The warmth of his embrace faded. She liked being close to him. Nearly dying in the freezer made her realize how much she'd missed out on in life. Some part of her had closed off and shut down after her parents and brother died. Her life had become about surviving. She didn't want to live that way anymore. She pushed herself off the floor and reached out to touch Jude's arm. Lacey felt as though she was on some kind of crazy roller coaster ride. She had no idea how to live differently. The irony was that now that she wanted a more abundant life, her physical well-being was under threat. Someone wanted her dead. "What do we do now?"

He turned to face her. "Are you hungry?

First of all, we should maybe go upstairs and find some food."

"I'm starving," she said.

He tilted his head toward the ceiling. "While we're up there, look closely at everybody around us. One of them could be the tall thin man. Try to remember anything you can."

Her stomach had tightened into a hard knot.

"Let's just be practical here, okay? We both need food in our bellies." He must have recognized the fear in her expression. His voice held a note of tenderness. "I'll stay near you."

"I didn't see him…at all this time." She wrapped her arms around her body, feeling herself going numb. She didn't want to think about any of this.

"Try to remember anything you can about today and last night's attack, a smell, an article of clothing." He touched her arm lightly at the elbow. "Food first. Let's go upstairs."

She managed a nod. Upstairs, most people had finished eating but many continued to sit and visit. The cacophony of voices made Lacey wince. Jude led her to a seat. He patted her shoulder. "You just sit. I'll get the food."

Lacey sat staring at the table, then she lifted her head and looked around. There were plenty of tall thin men. She saw the two hunters from the hotel. They nodded in recognition at her.

Jude set down a steaming bowl of soup in front of her along with a spoon, napkin and roll.

"They're out of the salad," he said.

He sat down beside her with his own bowl of soup.

She still didn't feel like her brain was working at a hundred percent. She studied Jude's face. Worry lines formed around his mouth and forehead. Much too intense for a man so young. Always, from the first time she'd met him, there was a warmth in his eyes that made her feel drawn to him. He wasn't wrong about her needing to stay close to him.

She tore the roll in half and dipped it in the soup. It tasted salty and comforting. She took several spoons full, relishing the warmth of it.

A man dressed in snow gear stepped up on the stage and tapped on a microphone that had been set up. The chatter in the room tapered off.

The man spoke in a clear voice. "I trust all of you have filled your bellies."

The people nodded and laughed.

"For the few of you who are not from Lodgepole I am the mayor. I've been in radio contact with the weather service and we are looking at two more days before the roads are passable by car at the very least."

Everyone groaned.

"If you are low on food or other cold weather supplies, please see my wife, Nancy, and she will issue you some. Another meal here at the school is planned for tomorrow. Right now, the most pressing thing is for us to check on the welfare of people in the cabins and homes outside the city. There may be people who need medical attention or food or they may not have heat. The roads should be passable by snowmobile. I need five sets of volunteers, two people in each team, to check on the residents and report back."

Jude perked up. He squeezed Lacey's shoulder. "We should do that."

His remark caught her off guard.

"I can't leave you here alone. It's not safe." He leaned closer and whispered in her ear. "I think the little girl might be in one of those houses that connects with that road."

"Okay." What else were they going to do, sit in their hotel room wrapped in blankets, watching in case someone tried to break in? Hang out with the townspeople so the attacker could have another crack at her? She was used to being outside in adverse conditions; she thrived on it. The safest place was with Jude.

They both raised their hands. The mayor nodded at them while several other people raised their hands, as well.

"Good, meet me back at my office in fifteen minutes. We'll get you suited up and ready to go."

She followed Jude out of the school into the whirling snow, realizing that a little girl's life might depend on what they found at the houses.

Jude only had to ask one person on the street to find out that the mayor's office was inside the bank because the mayor was also the bank manager. They hurried across town to the bank which had a single light on inside. The mayor came to the door and let them in.

"So glad you volunteered. You didn't have to, being from out of town and all." The mayor held out his hand. "I'm Lev Stevenson by the way."

There was another team of two men coming up the street, as well. One of them was tall and thin. Jude needed to make sure they searched the cabins on the mountain road where his car had been run off the road. "I'm a little bit familiar with this area. I've driven on Mountain Sun Road close to Shadow Ridge."

"You can have that area, then," said Lev. "Come with me." He led them to a back room that had snowsuits and helmets. "Find your size. The city owns several snowmobiles. They're in the back lot. I'll print out a list of the residences that connect with that road and the landmarks to look for. I'll show you where they are on a map, as well."

Lev pointed out that there were four homes on that road. Two that were occupied by locals and two that were seasonal cabins. The other two men came in and suited up. Jude watched Lacey shrink back.

"I don't know if either of those cabins were occupied at the time of the storm," said Lev.

One of those cabins had to be where the man was keeping Maria. Lev seemed like an honest man and he was not tall and thin, but he couldn't say anything to Lev while the two other men were within earshot. "We should be able to hit all four residences?"

"Weather and conditions permitting," said Lev.

Twenty minutes later, he and Lacey were suited up. Lev loaded a backpack of emergency supplies to the back of the snowmobile. He handed Lacey a radio as she got on behind Jude.

Several other teams had shown up, as well. Some were inside suiting up. Others already on their snowmobiles.

Lev pointed to the radio. "You can communicate for limited distances with that."

"Thanks," said Laccy as she put the radio in an inside pocket of the snowsuit. Both of them got into their helmets. Lev gave them a thumbs-up.

Lacey wrapped her arms around Jude and he took off on the snow-covered road. Snow had drifted across part of the road causing the snowmobile to bump along and catch air. Lacey held on even tighter.

Jude hoped that he had made the right decision. He couldn't wait until the roads were cleared to try to find Maria. Every second counted. Since he could not communicate with George Ignatius, he had no idea if the ransom demand had been made yet. Maybe he could find the little girl, break her out and get her to safety.

He hoped too that he had made the right decision for Lacey's safety. Staying back in town seemed to guarantee another attack. He suspected that it was just a matter of convenience to go after Lacey first at the school.

She was more vulnerable than him. The kidnapper and whomever his accomplice was sure didn't want him to solve this case.

Jude leaned forward, tucked in behind the snowmobile windshield as the cold stung the exposed part of his neck. The mountain road wound up and up. They passed the grove of trees where Lacey had parked her truck.

He twisted the throttle as the road became even more precarious. Lacey pressed in close and held on tight.

He slowed when they came to the place where his car had gone off the road. It was covered in drifts and barely visible. There were deep dents and grooves where he'd slid and then rolled over. He probably wouldn't be able to get it towed out until spring, the least of his worries.

He'd studied the map before taking off. This main mountain road connected with several spur roads where there were houses. He had an obligation to check on the residents, but what he really wanted to do was see if anyone was in the cabins. Someone could be up here for hunting season, but they could also be holding a little girl in one of them.

Up ahead, Jude spotted a handmade signpost, a piece of wood shaped like an arrow. The wood looked like it may have at one time had something painted on it, but it was now too faded to make out. That had to be the first spur road. Lev had said that an old man lived there by himself.

Jude took the turn on the road. The road wound through forest that grew denser cutting out much of the midday light. Up ahead he saw a house. There was no smoke coming out of the chimney and the windows were dark. Not a good sign.

He stopped the snowmobile twenty feet from the front door. Lacey got off first, and he followed. They pulled off their helmets. The wind chilled his skin.

"Let's hope he is open to having some visitors," said Jude.

"Let's hope he's okay," said Lacey.

They approached the dark house. Their boots crunched in the snow. Jude pulled his glove off, raised his hand and knocked on the door.

SEVEN

Lacey felt a tightening in her stomach as Jude pounded on the door. He pulled his hand away.

"What if he's...frozen or hurt?" She turned to look around the place. There was one car now half-covered in snow, and no sign of a snowmobile. The wind rustled through the upper branches of the pines. It sure was isolated out here.

Jude raised his fist and knocked again. The knocking seemed to echo. He stepped back, letting his hands fall at his sides.

His expression was pensive.

"We should probably check around the property before we try to get inside, don't you think?"

He put his finger to his lips indicating she needed to be quiet. "Do you hear that?"

She leaned toward the door, tilting her head. There was some sort of noise, far away but growing louder. Then she recognized it as the sound of several barking dogs. The barking increased in volume until they were right on the other side of the door.

"What did Lev say this guy's name was?"

"Mr. Wilson. Angus was his first name."

Jude stepped closer to the door and shouted to be heard above the dogs. "Mr. Wilson, are you in there? We're from Lodgepole. We've come to check that you are safe."

The dogs barked and then quieted. She could hear them moving around and whining.

Lacey pictured Mr. Wilson lying dead somewhere in the house.

"Mr. Wilson?"

A man came around from the side of the house dressed in coveralls, a knit cap and holding a rifle, which was aimed at them.

On impulse, Lacey threw her hands up. Her heart pounded wildly at the sight of the rifle.

Jude stepped in front of her. "Mr. Wilson?"

"Who wants to know?" the man said.

"We were sent from Lodgepole to check on your safety. We have a few supplies with us," Jude said.

The rifle went slack in the man's arms after he sized up Lacey and Jude. "I'm doing just fine. Sorry about the rifle. Some people use the storm for an opportunity to rob folks."

Jude thought Angus's place was a little bit inconveniently located for a robbery, but he understood the man's fear, being alone and older.

"Is there anything you need?" Lacey stepped toward him. "The house is dark and there was no smoke coming out of the chimney."

"I'm fine. I've been holed up in a little shed in the back that is easier to heat. I've got a little generator." Angus Wilson tilted his head toward the sky and then stared down his long road. "I imagine it will be a few more days before the plows get up this way."

"The mayor said it would take a couple days to open up the roads around town," Lacey said. "Are you sure there is nothing we can help you with?"

"Naw, I've lived here for forty years. Storms come and storms go. I'm prepared." Angus stepped toward the porch. The dogs were still making noise on the other side of the door.

Jude put a hand out to help Angus up the steps. "Mr. Wilson. I know there is one other occupied house that connects with that main road and some cabins that are often empty. I'm wondering if you've noticed any strange vehicles coming and going in the last few days when you were out on that main road."

Angus Wilson studied Jude for a long moment. "I ain't seen nothing strange. 'Course I mind my own business, which is what everyone should do."

Lacey felt like there was a warning in Angus's words.

"You don't know if anyone is in the cabins up the mountain and who they might be?"

"You ask a lot of questions," Angus said.

"Just want to make sure everyone is safe," Jude replied.

The old man shook his head. "Those folks who come up to the cabins are rarely very friendly to the locals."

The dogs continued to scratch and whine at the door. Angus opened it, so they could get out. He closed it quickly. "I left them in the main house. They were making me crazy in that little shed." There were three dogs: a border collie, a Lab-looking dog who moved like she was older and a white short-haired dog that must be some sort of pit bull cross.

Jude thanked the man, and he and Lacey returned to the snowmobile. Lacey grabbed her helmet, waving goodbye to Angus Wilson before getting on the snowmobile behind Jude. She wrapped her arms around his waist. He patted her gloved hand.

The gesture was one of familiarity. It

touched her heart. She felt so comfortable with him. Despite her resistance, they were growing closer. After she lost her family, she had dated some. Any time things seemed to be getting serious, she'd requested a research job that would take her to somewhere else. Forming attachments meant feeling pain. It would probably just be the same with Jude.

The snowmobile lurched to life and Jude got it turned around and headed back to the main road. He drove for a while before pulling onto a shoulder. She got off, wondering why he had stopped.

Jude dismounted as well and removed his helmet. He spread the map Lev had given them out on the seat of the snowmobile. He pointed to a spot on the map marked with an *X*. "That family we're supposed to check up on is way back here from the road. The cabins are directly off the main road but farther up. I feel like the clock is ticking. I have to know if that little girl is in one of those cabins. If she is up there, I might need your help extracting her." He stared at her for a long moment.

Lacey's heart skipped a beat as she considered the potential danger. Jude had protected her, she needed to be a support to him. "A little girl's life depends on us. I'm all in."

His features softened, and it was as if a light

had been sparked beneath his skin. He clamped a hand on her shoulder and squeezed. "Okay, good. Let's do this." Before he put his helmet on he turned back toward her. "Thank you."

Once they were on the snowmobile, Jude sped up the winding road through the deep snow. Lacey held on and prayed that the little girl would be brought home safe. If she was in one of those cabins, Lacey prayed she and Jude would be able to free her without losing their own lives.

Jude switched the headlights to the higher beam.

They had maybe three hours before it grew dark. They couldn't stay out here much past sunset. It would just be too hard to see potential hazards in the road.

Jude rounded a bend. He slowed. She peered over his shoulder. The intense headlights of another snowmobile filled her vision.

Jude slowed down even more. He waved.

The other driver did not wave back. It sped up, coming straight toward them. Lacey tensed as she held on to Jude and peered over his shoulder. Did this man mean to crash into them?

To avoid being hit, Jude performed a sharp turn. He was no longer on the road but headed cross-country.

As they turned, she got a look at the other snowmobile, not the same one that had come after them in town. This one had bright colors—orange, yellow and red.

Jude twisted the throttle. Lacey glanced over her shoulder. The other snowmobile was following them and closing the distance between them. They were being chased down.

Jude peered ahead. It was hard to read the terrain. The whiteness of the snow nearly blinded him even with the polarized visor of his helmet. If the sun had been at its apex, he might not be able to see anything. Though the helmet muffled the sound, he heard the roar of the other snowmobile intensify as it drew closer.

Because it was hard to see what was beneath the snow, there was a danger of hitting a rock or some other object that could catapult them off the snowmobile. He dared not slow down though. The other driver was bent on chasing them. This could only mean one thing—the girl must be in one of those cabins. Word must have gotten to the kidnapper that searchers would be out to check on people.

Jude checked his mirrors. The other driver was within feet of them. They bumped through some drifts, catching air and landing hard. Jude accidentally bit his tongue. He tasted blood. His heart pounded.

In his peripheral vision, he saw the lights of the other snowmobile. He had to do something radical to shake this guy.

He turned sharply, making his way down the mountain in a serpentine pattern until they were on the road again only lower on the mountain. The other snowmobile slipped in behind him though he'd managed to put some distance between them.

He veered off the road and into a grove of trees praying there would be a way through. Once he was hidden by the trees, he switched off his headlight and slowed down to a crawl. The snowmobile putted along until there was no visible way through other than going back the way they'd come. Even then, getting turned around would be a challenge. He switched off the engine.

Lacey flipped up her helmet and he did the same. They could hear the other snowmobile circling around. He hadn't followed them into the dense forest probably fearing an ambush or getting stuck.

The other snowmobile sounded like it was idling.

"Do you think he's going to wait for us to come out?"

"I doubt he'll come on foot in here to find us. We'd have the upper hand unless he is armed." There was a high probability of that since they were probably dealing with the same man who had shot at Jude with a rifle. Jude turned in a half circle studying the thickness of the trees. "This was a big section of the forest. He can't watch every inch of this forest."

The other snowmobile was back in motion accelerating, circling around the grove of trees. The engine noise grew louder, then dimmed and grew louder again.

"Maybe we can find another way out," Lacey said.

While the other snowmobile continued to run patrol, they searched the forest for a clear path. Jude found a sort of trail where the trees were not as thick. From where he stood, he could see the edge of the forest.

Lacey stood beside him. "Do you think the snowmobile can fit through there?"

"It's our only choice," Jude said. "We can't hope to escape on foot. Come on, let's clear some of this brush and get back to the snowmobile."

Once they were on the snowmobile, Jude

looked down at the gas gauge. Escaping the other snowmobile had used up a lot of fuel. Even if they could shake their pursuer, there wouldn't be enough fuel to get up to those cabins and back to town. Frustration caused a tightening through his chest.

Lacey spoke over his shoulder. "You all right?"

"Let's head back to town before we run out of gas." Being stranded on the mountain with a kidnapper nipping at their heels would not do anyone any good.

He started the snowmobile but kept the headlight turned off. He maneuvered through the narrow path. He cranked the throttle to get over a mound of snow. Up ahead, he could see the fading daylight and an opening through the trees.

Jude took in a deep breath. He couldn't hear the other snowmobile at all. But that didn't mean it wasn't close. They came to the edge of the trees. He sped up, zooming out into the open. He looked side to side not seeing the other driver.

He had to get back up to the road. He circled around the trees. Lacey held on tight as the snowmobile climbed up the hill. The terrain was rough. The engine revved and groaned as they navigated around the drifts and snow-covered bumps that might be rocks or fallen logs.

The landscape evened out. He took in a breath when he saw the road up ahead. Lacey pounded on his shoulder. In his mirror he saw the other snowmobile some distance behind them but closing in. The kidnapper must have been waiting for them on the road.

Jude sped up as the other driver drew closer. Jude went even faster, rounding a curve at a dangerous speed. The sparse lights of Lodgepole came into view. Almost there. He looked behind. No sign of the other snowmobile.

They rumbled along the road and he relaxed a little.

His snowmobile clanged and sputtered. When he looked down, the gas gauge read Empty.

EIGHT

Even before the snowmobile came to a complete stop, Lacey knew they were out of gas. Jude swung off the snowmobile and tore off his helmet. He glanced nervously up the road.

She didn't see any sign of the other vehicle. Could they hope that he had given up the chase because they were so close to town? That seemed unlikely.

He tugged on Lacey's jacket while she was pulling her helmet off her head. "You have the radio?"

She nodded and placed a gloved palm on her chest where the hard plastic had dug into her skin.

"Let's hide in the trees. Hopefully we're close enough to town to be able to call for help."

Heart racing, Lacey zipped open the backpack and grabbed a packet of food which she slipped into her coat pocket. She took the food on instinct. She didn't know if they would be out here for only a short time or if they would be dodging the man on the snowmobile for hours and walking back to town.

"Come on, hurry." He grabbed her hand and they raced toward the trees.

Their footsteps made almost a mushy sound in the soft snow. Her boot sunk down deep. Progress was slow. Jude held on to her hand.

The trees loomed up ahead. She thought she heard the sound of a motor but couldn't be sure. They entered the forest and kept running. Lacey took in jagged cold breaths as her legs grew tired. Jude kept going. They were moving farther and farther away from the road.

Jude came to an abrupt stop. They were far enough in that they couldn't see the road anymore. She pulled the radio out of her chest pocket and clicked it on. The green light glowed. She prayed they would be able to reach someone. She pressed the talk button and cleared her throat. "This is Snow Team One. Is anyone there?" She let up on the button, feeling the tension coil inside her belly.

"Try again," said Jude.

She pressed the button. "This is Snow Team One. We need help." She let up on the button, hearing only static.

Though the sound was faint, she could

hear a snowmobile putting along and then stopping. The kidnapper was out there probably looking at their snowmobile. Their boot tracks into the forest would be easy enough to follow. Her breath caught in her throat. The man had a rifle. He'd used it before on them when Jude had wrecked his car. She hadn't gotten a good enough look to know if he had a rifle with him now. He hadn't come after them before when they'd hidden in the trees. Maybe he wasn't armed.

A voice came across the line. "Snow Team One. This is Lev. What's your problem?"

Lacey breathed a sigh of relief at the sound of Lev's voice. "We've run out of gas. I don't know exactly where we are, but we can see the lights of Lodgepole, what there is of them."

"I can send someone up with gas to get you home."

"That sounds good. There's something else." She looked at Jude, not sure how much she was supposed to tell.

Jude took the radio. "Listen, someone has been after us, chasing us. It's not safe for us to wait by the snowmobile and you need to approach with caution. He's dangerous."

Static came across the line. Lev was probably trying to process what he'd just been told. "Don't worry about us. Some of us will be armed. So…how will we find you?"

Lacey was glad Lev didn't ask too many questions. He was just focused on getting people home safe.

Jude pressed the button. "We'll listen for the sound of your snowmobile approaching. We'll come out of the trees then."

"Okay, we're losing daylight here. How many houses did you get to?"

"Only one, Mr. Wilson is okay."

"We'll send you or another team out again tomorrow," Lev said. "Hold tight. We'll be up there as fast as we can."

Jude pushed the disconnect button and handed the radio back to Lacey. "At least we know we can trust Lev. He's too large to be the guy who attacked you in your room. Now I'm thinking maybe we should let him in on the possibility that Maria is being held somewhere around here."

Lacey gestured toward the road. "Do you think it's safe just to wait here?"

"I don't know. He must know we're hiding in the trees."

"I was thinking if he has a gun, he might come in after us," she said.

"Let's keep moving. We're going to have to

get closer to the road to hear that snowmobile coming from Lodgepole."

"If the driver leaves right away, it will take at least twenty minutes for him to get up here."

Some distance through the trees, Lacey heard the sound of a branch breaking. Her heart stopped, and her breath caught.

Jude must have heard it too. He gestured for them to move deeper into the trees. The noise could be an animal or the wind. But they couldn't take any chances.

They stepped cautiously, trying not to make noise. If the kidnapper had been close by, he would have heard them talking on the radio. As they moved, Lacey studied the trees. She squinted to discern shadow from substance in the dim light of evening.

Jude seemed to be moving in a sort of arc that would lead them back to the road. They stopped where the canopy of the evergreens cut out nearly all the remaining daylight.

She pressed her back against a tree trunk. She glanced at Jude who seemed to be tuned in to his surroundings. They dared not speak and give away their position.

She listened as well and studied the trees for any sign of movement. All of her senses were heightened. Her heart pounded. She heard the creaking of tree branches as the scent of pine filled her nose. She tasted fear, metallic and cold. She tensed up, ready to run if she had to.

A growling stomach caused her to touch her belly, afraid that even that noise would tell their pursuer where they were.

She pulled the food packet out of her pocket. She had to remove her glove to open it. The chill stung her fingers. She opened the packet slowly and handed a piece of the protein bar to Jude who nodded a thank-you.

They hadn't heard the sound of a snowmobile starting up, which meant their pursuer was out there watching and waiting or he was searching the forest for them. Either way, he was still a threat.

Once they had eaten their food, Jude gestured for her to follow him. He worked his way back toward the edge of the forest. As the trees thinned, the setting sun shed light on them. Jude came within a few feet of where the evergreens no longer grew. He slipped behind a tree with a thick trunk and peered out.

She chose a tree that provided her with a view of the road. Their snowmobile was parked there in the middle of the road. About ten feet away and off on a shoulder was their pursuer's snowmobile. The man who had chased them down was nowhere in sight. Was he searching for them? Or had he taken up a position with his rifle, ready to shoot as soon as they came out into the open?

A gust of wind sent a miniature tornado of snow toward them. She closed her eyes and shrank back behind the tree. Both of them pressed their backs against their respective trees. Waiting. Listening. She was not able to get a deep breath.

Jude turned his head so he was looking at her. She couldn't see his expression clearly. He shrugged his shoulders and shook his head.

Would the sound of the snowmobile from town approaching be enough to scare their pursuer away, or would the kidnapper see their rescuer as collateral damage and take him out too?

Having to be still and wait with danger so close by was harder than running. She was aware of her heartbeat drumming in her ears and the tightness through her chest.

Then she heard it. The faint and faraway sound of a snowmobile drawing closer. She let out a heavy breath. Jude rose to his feet. She did the same but remained with her back pressed against the tree.

Then they heard the sound of another

snowmobile starting up and fading. The kidnapper was leaving. She pushed off the tree. Jude reached out a gloved hand to grab hers.

She supposed it was a natural protective gesture. He didn't mean anything by it. Still, it was a reminder of the affection that had blossomed between them and that she felt herself draw away from. The approaching snowmobile grew louder. They headed down the snowy bank and stepped out onto the road just as headlights became visible around a curve.

She glanced up the road and didn't see the pursuer's snowmobile. But if she tuned in to the noises around her, she thought she detected the distant sound of an engine as the kidnapper's vehicle drew farther away.

She turned her attention to the approaching snowmobile. A spark of fear surged through her. The driver was tall and thin. She reached out for Jude's hand.

His posture stiffened, as well. He squeezed her hand. "We don't know anything yet. We have to get back to town."

The driver came to a stop but left his snowmobile idling.

Lacey pressed her lips together as the driver tore off his helmet. She relaxed. It wasn't a he at all. The driver was a tall thin lady with gray hair pulled back in a ponytail. "I got some gas for you folks," she said, turning toward the container she had strapped on the back of her snowmobile.

Jude stepped out toward the woman and took the gas can. "Thank you."

The woman tilted her head toward the darkening sky. "We better hurry. Don't have much daylight left. I'll wait to make sure your snowmobile starts up. I'm Nancy by the way. Lev's wife."

Lacey stepped toward the older woman. "Nice to meet you." She held out a gloved hand. There was something trustworthy in Nancy's expression.

Nancy pointed at the rifle she had mounted on the snowmobile. "Lev said there might be trouble. Over his objections, I volunteered. I'm the best shot in town, almost made the Olympic team as a biathlete when I was younger."

Jude poured the gas into the tank and started up the snowmobile. He gave Nancy the thumbs-up.

She nodded and gave him the thumbs-up. "Stop by the bank when you get into town. Leave the snowmobile there. Pop your head in. Lev wants to make sure you made it back safe."

"Got it," said Jude.

Nancy got back on her snowmobile, zoomed a ways up the road until she found a wide spot to turn around and then headed back down the mountain. She disappeared around the curve just as Lacey and Jude got into their helmets.

Jude stared down at his gauges. "Looks like just enough gas to get us back into town."

"That's the plan, right?"

Jude glanced up the road where the kidnapper had sped away. "That little girl must be in one of those cabins. We have to get to her…somehow."

Lacey couldn't argue with him.

"I'm going to take you back into town and then I'm going to see if I can talk to Lev. I'll let him know the whole story. See if he is open to going out with me to search the cabins."

"It'll be dark soon." Even as she spoke, she knew she couldn't argue with him. This was a child they were talking about.

"I know navigating at night has more hazards, but I don't think we can wait."

Jude got on the snowmobile and Lacey slipped in behind him. He twisted the throttle and sped down the road. She rested her head against Jude's shoulder, feeling the fatigue settle into her muscles. She knew that she didn't have the energy to brave the cold and the dark again. That meant she would be left alone while Jude went out. She didn't much care for that idea either.

Jude was not wrong. Time was of the essence in finding Maria. Still, the thought of being alone in Lodgepole struck a chord of terror inside her.

Jude was glad to see the lights of the town grow closer though they were much sparser than the last time they'd come into Lodgepole. Up ahead, he saw Nancy's taillights as she came to the edge of town and turned off on a side street.

Much of the snow had been removed from Main Street.

He wrestled with the choices that lay ahead for him. To leave Lacey behind meant she might be in danger. But he couldn't wait until morning to search the cabins where Maria might be held.

Even through the padding of his snowsuit, he could feel the weight of Lacey resting against his shoulder. She might already be asleep.

He pulled up by the bank where there were still lights on inside. He could just make out Lev's silhouette as he stood watching. As they stopped and pulled helmets off, Lev came to the door and held it open for them. "Glad to see you made it. You're the last team to come back."

Jude stepped toward the warmth of the building. "Sir, I need to talk to you."

Lev's shoulders drooped. He was probably tired too. "Come on in."

Lacey followed behind.

He turned to face her. "I'm not sure what to do. I don't think going back to the hotel will be safe for you."

"I'd rather stay with you until I know what the plan is."

Jude felt like his insides were being ripped apart. He didn't blame her for being afraid to be alone. "Maybe we can ask Lev if you can stay at his place. You'd be safe there."

She nodded. "You must be tired too."

He was exhausted but that didn't matter.

Lev ushered them into the back room where they could get out of their snowsuits. A lantern had been set up to provide some light. He'd seen some lights on in town but not many. Maybe people had backup generators.

Lev sat on the bench.

Jude took in a deep breath and explained everything. That Maria was probably in one of the unoccupied cabins. That he had been unable to communicate with Maria's father,

George Ignatius. That he had no idea what the kidnapper might do. He told Lev about the attempts on his and Lacey's lives while they had been in Lodgepole as well as while they were on the mountain. "So you see, Lev, I've got to go back up there. And I need to go with someone I can trust. This can't wait."

Lev rubbed his chin. He stared at Jude for a long moment. "You're not going back up there in the dark."

"But, sir..."

Lev raised his hand. "You're exhausted. You'll end up having an accident. I will search the cabins with some men I trust. You and Lacey can stay at my house with Nancy."

Even as Lev spoke, Jude knew he didn't have the energy to make it back up that mountain. Lev was right. He'd end up wrecking the snowmobile or worse. Lev gave them the directions to his house. "If you run into the man who is holding her, there might be violence."

"I have a gun," said Lev. "I can radio Nancy and let her know you are coming over." He patted Jude on the shoulder. "Get some sleep."

Jude nodded. Still, his guts felt tied up in knots. Staying with Nancy was safer than being at the hotel and at least he could stay close to Lacey. "Wake me as soon as you get back into town."

Lev nodded. "I'll get up there as fast as I can. I just need to find someone to man the radio for me."

He and Lacey headed out to Main Street. All the windows in the businesses were dark. They turned onto the side street and no one was walking around. The quiet hush offered a sort of comfort. They found Lev's house. Nancy stood at the window, looking out as they made their way up the snowy walk.

She opened the door for them and welcomed them. "Come on in."

They stepped inside. There was a fire going in the woodstove that made the living room toasty warm. The furniture was rustic in style with lots of natural wood and leather. The lights on the wall must have been battery operated.

Nancy gripped her bathrobe at the neck. "I'm afraid I have limited things to offer. We are trying to ration our use of the generator. I can warm you up some water on the cookstove if you want a hot beverage."

Lacey glanced over at him. "I think we both would just like to get some sleep."

Nancy pointed toward the woodstove. "The warmest place is in the living room. I've made up the couch and I was just going to grab a pad and a sleeping bag. Be right back."

"You can have the couch," Jude said.

She smiled faintly. "Thanks."

Her expression brought back some of the warmth and good feelings he'd had when they'd first met. He shook his head. He'd come to Montana to do a job. Maybe that was where he needed to keep his focus.

Lacey took her boots off and placed them beside the couch. She lay down on the couch, adjusted the pillow and pulled the blankets around her, staring at the fire through the glass door of the woodstove.

Nancy returned and handed Jude the bedding. "You don't want to sleep too close to the stove, you will wake up in a pool of sweat. I'll try to have some breakfast for you in the morning."

Jude thanked Nancy. She nodded and disappeared down a hallway.

Lacey had closed her eyes. He laid out the pad and sleeping bag. A noise outside alerted him. He rose to his feet. The window that faced the backyard looked out on a road. Three snowmobiles sped by. That had to be Lev and whoever he had recruited to search the cabins in the dark.

His stomach twisted into tight knots. He wasn't sure if he'd even be able to sleep until he knew what the men found. He glanced over at Lacey whose relaxed posture indicated she had fallen asleep.

Still restless, Jude moved around the room making sure the doors were locked. At least he could keep Lacey safe tonight. He settled down on the pad, unzipped the down sleeping bag and crawled inside. He set his gun off to one side but within reach. He stared at the ceiling for a long moment trying to pray. The prayer on the mountain when he was being shot at had been out of total desperation.

Though he was not in danger or in fear of losing his life, a sense of desperation invaded his mind. Desperation for Maria to be returned safely to her parents, and for him to feel like he'd redeemed himself from ten years ago.

He pulled the sleeping bag up close to his neck. The down surrounded his body and warmed him. He struggled to make the words of the prayer form. Did he only need God if he thought he was going to die? His faith had been so solid at one point in his life.

Lacey rolled over, so she was facing the back of the couch.

He listened to the gentle sound of her breathing.

If he was totally honest with himself, he wished too that there could be something between him and Lacey. He loved her easy laugh and the way her face got all animated when she talked about her work. But what did he have to offer her? He was a washed-up cop with only a fraction of the faith she displayed.

He stared at the ceiling, not able to form the words of a prayer but knowing that God understood anyway. His eyelids grew heavy, and he drifted off to sleep.

Hours later, his eyes fluttered open. Though he could not tell if he had dreamed it or if it was really happening, he thought he'd heard noises. He sat up. Alarmed, he rose to his feet. From what he could see, Lacey was not on the couch. The blanket that had covered her lay on the floor. Panic spread through his body as his senses tried to absorb what was happening.

It was still night outside. His eyes had not adjusted to the dark room. He heard muffled noises. As he glanced across the floor, he could see only shadows. He ran toward the noise in the next room just in time to see a dark figure unlock the back door in the kitchen from the inside and swing it open. The man disappeared into the darkness and he had Lacey with him.

Jude stepped into the first pair of shoes he saw. They were too big for him. The move had cost him precious seconds, but he wouldn't get far barefoot. He yelled once for Nancy to come help him. He didn't have time to find her room in the house.

A cold wind hit him as he stepped outside to search. In the dark, he could just make out boot tracks and two parallel lines. Signs of a barefoot Lacey being dragged away.

How could anyone know they were even here instead of at the hotel unless they'd been followed from the bank?

Someone had gotten to Lacey, probably taking her to a quiet place where killing her couldn't be heard.

NINE

Cold seeped into Lacey's bare feet as she struggled to get away from her abductor. Everything had happened so fast. A few minutes before in the house, the man had put a gun to her head probably intending to kill both her and Jude while they slept. She had managed to knock the gun out of his hand. Jude had seen she was being taken. He couldn't be far behind.

Her kidnapper still held a hand over her mouth and the other suctioned around her waist as he dragged her through the snow. The chill seeped through her thin layer of clothes. She tried to get traction with her feet but to no avail. She twisted her head and torso to break free. She fell on the cold ground in a heap.

She couldn't see the house. Her kidnapper had dragged her behind a bunch of trees.

Her abductor grabbed her by the collar and

lifted her up. Already she was shivering. She reached out toward his face. He was wearing a ski mask. He was tall and thin. Again, he wrapped his arms around her waist.

"Jude…somebody," she tried to yell, but her voice was paper thin.

He clasped a gloved hand over her mouth. "Be quiet!" His voice held a note of rage that scared her even more. She had no doubt that his intent was to kill her.

As he continued to drag her through the snow, she spied the backyards of the houses on the same street they had searched. The run-down blue Victorian house was set off from the others. The tall thin man must be looking for a hiding place to kill her before Jude found them. When she looked where they had been, she saw no sign of Jude. The back sides of the houses looked very far away.

She had to get away. His grip around her waist was like iron. He swung her around and planted her feet. He gripped her wrist. "We need to run." He yanked her arm, pulling her through a cluster of trees. They ran for at least five minutes before he stopped. She stood before a set of stairs leading to a door that belonged to what looked like a single wide trailer. The trailer was off by itself, and it was not visible through the trees.

"Get in," he barked.

Her heartbeat drummed in her ears. Once she was inside, she was a dead woman. She turned and took off running. Her bare feet sunk down in the snow, chilling her to the bone. She took five steps before he was on top of her, tackling her to the ground. Her stomach pressed into the snow.

He rolled off of her. "Get up."

In what felt like one swift motion, he pulled her to her feet and pushed her into the trailer. Though she could not see much in the dark space, it was clear the trailer hadn't been occupied for some time. The place smelled like dust and mold. Cupboard doors hung on single hinges and what she could make out of the furniture, lopsided chairs and a couch with no cushions, indicated no one lived here.

She gripped the corner of the counter. He pushed on her back from behind. She took a step and felt a sting to her foot.

She lifted her leg. "I think I cut myself."

He pushed her again. "Like it's going to matter."

She limped forward. The house was nothing more than shadows. But there had to be a back door. She bolted down the hall as pain from the cut shot up her leg. The fact that her feet were already cold numbed some of the potential pain.

Because of all the junk and broken furniture, the house was like a maze. She crashed into furniture. She ran into a room and flipped open a window, preparing to crawl out.

He found her and pulled her back in. He pushed her to the ground and his arms were around her neck. He squeezed tight as she struggled for breath.

Her hands reached out for something... anything. Fingers wrapped around an object, something metal. She lifted it and hit him in the back. The blow was enough to make him let go of her and cry out in pain. She rolled away and scrambled to her feet, hitting him again but this time in the shoulder. She ran down the hallway.

Please, God, let there be a back door here.

She saw it then at the other end of the trailer, a door swinging on its hinges. She stepped through it expecting stairs. Instead she found herself falling through space and landing on the ground. Her knees hit first and then her hands.

Behind her, she could hear the noise of her abductor crashing through the trailer.

She rose to her feet and started to run, back

toward Nancy's house, back toward safety. But she was disoriented. She'd run in the wrong direction and now she was surrounded by trees. She turned in a circle, trying to get her bearings.

A voice came to her ears, calling her name. Somewhere out in the darkness. It was Jude.

"I'm here. Jude." Her voice sounded faint and far away like it hadn't even come out of her throat. She hurried toward the sound of his voice.

She glanced over her shoulder as she ran. Where had the tall thin man gone?

Jude was suddenly there. Out of breath, she pressed herself against his chest. He wrapped his arms around her. "It's all right. I've got you."

"Do you see him back by that trailer?"

Jude still held her but lifted his head and turned slightly. "He's gone. He must have run off when he saw me coming toward you."

She felt both relief and rage. Relief that she was safe for now but rage that he was still out there in the shadows, waiting for another chance to come after her.

"Let's get you back to the house." Jude squeezed her shoulder.

She took a step forward her leg collapsed under her. Her feet were numb from the cold, and one of them was bleeding.

Jude looked down at her feet. "You're in no condition to walk." He swept her up in his arms and carried her toward the house.

She nestled her face close to his neck, breathing in the scent of wood smoke and musk. Her hand rested on his chest. She could feel herself getting light-headed. It wasn't entirely because of her injuries. Being held by Jude's strong arms made her feel like she was a balloon floating on the air.

She heard Nancy's voice. "Oh my, let's get her inside and warmed up." Though Lacey didn't think she'd managed to make much noise, Nancy must have been awakened. Maybe Jude had yelled for her help.

A door creaked open. Jude's boots made a different sound as they pounded across the wood floor. Nancy said something about heating up water and getting a first aid kit. Jude gently placed her on the couch. He grabbed the blanket and lifted it, so it covered her shoulders.

He kneeled and looked at her feet, then rubbed her uninjured foot between his hands.

"I can't see very well. Are your toes tingling?"

"No, just numb." She could feel the warmth of his fingers as he squeezed her foot. "I don't think I have frostbite. I'm just very cold." She drew the blankets even tighter around herself.

"You're probably right." He lifted her other foot. "It's this one I'm worried about. It looks like you have a cut on the side of it."

Nancy arrived with the hot water and first aid kit. "Let me get a lamp so you can see better." Lacey listened to her footsteps pad away and then return. "I'll hold the light." She brought it down closer to where Jude held her injured foot.

He washed her foot with warm water. The gentle touch soothed her. As the memory of the attack encroached, she was able to stay calm.

His finger pressed into the bottom of her foot. "You must have scraped it on something." He pulled something out of the first aid kit. "I need to disinfect it. It's going to sting a little."

"I can take it." She pressed her lips together.

"I know you can. You're one strong lady." He winked at her.

His playfulness sent a wave of electricity through her despite the pain she was in.

He pressed his thumb into the bottom of her foot and squeezed out the disinfectant. A sharp pain played across her nerves and then dissipated.

"Got it," he said.

"I think there's a bandage in there too," said Nancy.

Lacey closed her eyes as he pressed the bandage on.

"Is she going to be all right, Doctor?" Nancy's tone was joking.

"Yes, Nurse Nancy."

Lacey rested her hand on her chest, finally able to take a deep breath.

"I'm a little worried that man might come back." Nancy gripped her bathrobe at the neck.

"I'll make sure the house is secure and I'll stand watch until Lev gets back. Get some sleep, Nancy," Jude said.

After a moment's hesitation and nervous glance toward the kitchen, Nancy disappeared down the hallway.

Lacey could feel the heaviness of fatigue and the fallout from her attack weighing her muscles down.

"Why don't you try to sleep too." Jude stood up. "I'm going to make sure that window can't be opened again."

Lacey lay her head on the pillow and pulled her legs up toward her chest. She could hear Jude rooting around and then there was the sound of a hammer. By the time he returned, she was half-asleep.

She opened one eye. Jude had settled down on the pad and pulled the sleeping bag around himself while he stared at the fire in the woodstove.

"It's okay, you know," she said. "There's probably no way you could have prevented that guy coming in here."

"I should have stayed awake. I shouldn't have let my guard down. The reason why he's after you is because of me. Because you helped me."

"You were as tired out as I was." Even as she spoke, she could feel the tension between them again. It seemed that guilt ruled much of Jude's life. He must have felt a huge sense of responsibility ten years ago. That it was his job to save the husband and wife and now this kidnapped girl. "Jude, you're not invincible. You need sleep too. I know you would have prevented that guy from coming in here if you could have."

"I shouldn't have been sleeping so deeply."

"You're a human being. You need to eat and sleep like the rest of us. I'm just glad you came for me when you did. So quit beating yourself up…over everything."

He took a long moment to answer. "Okay." His tone suggested he didn't really mean what he said.

She pulled the blanket up toward her neck and stared at the ceiling. It seemed as though

Jude had carried the weight of the world on his shoulders for a long time. Would he ever forgive himself for what had happened ten years ago? "I know that you did everything that you could with that husband and wife. You always do the right thing. You're a good man, but that doesn't mean bad things won't happen."

Jude didn't answer for several moments. "You might be right. I never thought about it that way."

Lacey drifted off to sleep not knowing if her words had made a difference. She awoke hours later to the sound of heavy pounding on the front door.

Jude had only been half-asleep when he heard someone knocking at the door. He doubted the assailant would try to come back a second time and he certainly wouldn't knock.

Jude jumped to his feet just as Lacey opened her eyes. He peered through the window of the door. Lev stood outside in his full snowsuit gear but holding his helmet. Jude unlatched the door, feeling a tightness in his chest. It was just Lev on the front steps. No other searchers. No Maria.

Jude clicked back the dead bolt and twisted

the doorknob. Early morning sun shone in his eyes.

"Forgot my key," Lev said as he stepped inside. "We usually don't have to lock our doors."

"What did you find?" Fear zinged through him like a Ping-Pong ball. He prayed Maria hadn't been killed or left to die.

Lev placed his helmet on the table by the door. He turned to face Jude. "Nothing."

"Nobody was up there?"

"There was evidence in the vacation rental that someone had been there recently. The other place was locked up tight. I don't think anyone has been there in months."

Jude tried to process what Lev was telling him. Lacey sat up on the couch, stretching and yawning. Maybe the kidnapper had panicked and moved Maria from the vacation rental. But where would he go? His travel would be as limited as theirs was. The roads were still not plowed.

Lev pulled off his gloves. "Did you two get some rest?"

"We had a little excitement here. Someone got into the house and grabbed Lacey."

Lev looked at Jude and then at Lacey who had risen to her feet. "I'm sorry about that. You know, there are men in this town I trust with my life. We can start questioning guys who are tall and thin…maybe get to the bottom of this before the sheriff shows up."

"I don't want the whole town knowing what is going on. The tall thin man would probably just go into hiding," Jude said. "There is one more home to visit on that mountain road. I can go up there and check it out and then I need to take the time to look around myself. That car that was used to kidnap Maria was on that road for a reason."

"You can't go up there alone," Lev said.

"Lacey's foot is hurt, so she might need to stay here with someone watching her."

Lacey stepped toward them, favoring her cut foot only slightly. "It doesn't hurt that bad. I'd rather be helpful and go back out with Jude. I'm in danger no matter what. Might as well make myself useful. I feel safest when I'm with Jude." She stared at him with those wide round eyes.

Jude appreciated the vote of confidence, but he'd already messed up once. "Are you sure?"

She nodded.

Her words from the night before came back to him. Did he allow himself to be a human being who made mistakes? His intention was always to do the right thing. That had been his intention ten years ago. He had asked

God a thousand times why things had gone so wrong.

"I don't know if I like this plan." Lev shook his head. "It concerns me that that man came into my home and grabbed Lacey. I think maybe we should have her under some protection."

Lacey touched her hand to her chest. "Lev, I don't know if the man who came after me is someone from Lodgepole or an outsider who is in hiding. You're a good guy and I am sure most of the people in Lodgepole are good people, but right now Jude is the only one I trust."

Jude studied Lacey for a moment. Morning light from the window gave her auburn hair a golden tone. She wanted to be with him, if only for safety. She believed in him even if he didn't believe in himself.

Lev took a moment to answer. "It's your call, Lacey." He turned to face Jude. "I assume you carry a gun for your line of work."

Jude padded his chest.

"Okay, you can go up there again. Make sure when you take one of the town snowmobiles that you are fully fueled up."

"We'll grab some breakfast and head out so we have the full day. No need to wake Nancy. We can find something to eat," Jude said.

"I'd appreciate it. I'm pretty worn-out my-self. I need to get a couple hours shut-eye before I deal with everything that has to be done." Lev nodded and disappeared down the hallway.

Lacey and Jude ate from the food supply that Nancy had set out on the counter. She heated some water for oatmeal and instant coffee. She handed him one of the steaming mugs after she'd stirred the coffee in.

"Not exactly a mocha with whipped cream, but it will warm your belly and give you some energy," she said.

"I'm sure my stomach will say thank you." He lifted the steamy mug in a toast.

While they sipped the coffee, Lacey got the map out that Lev had given them with the house that needed to be checked in on. She laid it out on the table and pointed. "That last house is the farthest away from the main road. It will take a while to get to."

"Yes, that's the one where that family lives off the grid. Lev said we'd have to park the snowmobile and hike in."

The both stared at the map. "Besides those two cabins, there are no other residences that connect with that mountain road." Jude shook his head. "It doesn't make any sense. Where would he have taken her? He was on that road for some reason."

She pointed at the map. There are primitive roads that go off toward the other side of the mountain. "Maybe he was holding her on the other side of the mountain and going the long way to avoid detection."

"I don't know," Jude said. "I just know I have to keep trying."

They both stepped into the living room where they'd tossed their snowsuits and other winter gear. While they suited up they continued to talk.

"Maybe she was never in the cabin." Lacey sat down to pull on her boots after she'd zipped her suit up.

"Then why was he so bent on me not making it up that mountain road in the first place?"

She shook her head. "I don't know. Maybe he has a camper up there."

They stepped outside into the crisp clear morning. For the first time in days they could see blue sky even though the temperature felt like it might be hovering around zero.

"Just a second." Jude pulled his cell phone out. "I think I have a signal. I have to call George Ignatius. At least try to make contact. I'm sure he's sitting in his home in North

Dakota worried to death about his missing daughter."

Lacey nodded, sat sideways on the snowmobile and tilted her head toward the sun.

The phone rang several times. He heard a man's voice on the other end of the line. "George? It's Jude Trainor."

George's voice faded in and out. Jude thought he asked if Maria had been found yet.

"No, but I think she is being kept somewhere on Shadow Ridge. Has a ransom demand been made yet?"

A blast of static hit his ear. He thought he heard George say "Yes." And then all he could hear was warbled speech. "George, I can't hear you." He listened a moment longer before giving up.

They got onto the snowmobile, which revved to life. They refueled at the grain silo, where Lev had told them they would find some gas pumps, and headed back up the mountain.

The sun shining somehow renewed his hope and energy. They had at least eight hours before it got dark. It wouldn't take that long to check on the last home. He didn't doubt that Lev had not seen anyone at either of the cabins, but maybe there was some clue that would tell him that Maria had been there.

The snowmobile wound up the mountain past the first turnoff where they had checked on the old man and his dogs. They came to a fork in the road. He slowed the snowmobile and turned. He'd traveled maybe a quarter mile before the road became a trail.

The deadfall of forest and the heavy snow made it clear that if they tried to go any farther, they'd just end up getting stuck. He stopped the snowmobile.

Lacey got off first, grabbing the backpack that contained emergency supplies. Jude pulled his helmet off and looked around. "How crazy does someone have to be to live in such a remote place?"

"Lev didn't warn us in any way about them. Some people just don't want to be all caught up in modern life. I like it when my research takes me up to a cabin or campsite where I can't see the light of civilization anywhere, only the stars. It has its appeal."

There was a heaviness to her words. They had both been hiding, running for years just in different ways. "I suppose we all need to get away now and then." He reached toward her. "I'll carry the backpack."

He slipped into it and led the way through the trees. After a while, there was no clear path. They stepped around fallen logs and pushed the branches of bent-over trees out of the way.

He smelled wood smoke but couldn't see anything through the thick undergrowth. They stepped into the clearing where the smoke from a chimney twirled through the blue sky.

Lacey stepped forward and stood beside him. "That's a good sign. They are able to keep their house heated."

He liked that she stood so close to him. "I'm glad you decided to come out here with me."

"Honestly, Jude, I meant it. Being with you is the safest place for me."

"Thanks." He reached out and squeezed her gloved hand. Jude turned his attention back to the smoke though the house was still not visible. "Let's go make sure this family is okay."

If everything went according to plan, they would have plenty of time to search the area for any clues as to what had happened to Maria. He could not accept that she had never been on the mountain at all.

The kidnapper or kidnappers had communicated with George to set a ransom. If the kidnappers had demanded cash, assuming that Maria was being kept somewhere on the mountain, the exchange couldn't happen until the roads were open. That meant Maria was still alive. It also meant time was running out to find her.

TEN

Lacey heard the sound of children laughing even before she saw the house that belonged to the Johnsons. The forest thinned, and a structure that looked like it had been made from recycled materials came into view. Part of the dwelling was an old bus with rooms and walls extending out from it. Though the place looked like square footage had been added as needed, it was probably quite large inside.

Two boys, one maybe eight years of age and a teenager, threw snowballs at each other while a brown dog leaped in the air at the snowballs and yipped. The boys stopped and stared at Lacey and Jude when they stepped free of the trees.

Jude waved. "We're from Lodgepole. We're here to check on your safety."

The younger boy spoke up. "I'll get my

dad." He ran, disappearing around the side of the house.

The older boy picked up an ax and chopped wood while Lacey and Jude drew closer.

Lacey stepped toward the teenager who brought the ax down on a log. "Is everyone here okay?"

"We've been fine. Dad reckons we'll be able to dig out of here in a couple of days."

Several more children came to the window and looked out. Two girls and a blond baby who sucked his fingers as they watched with interest.

A man who looked like the teenager, only with a mustache, came around the corner of the house. He held out his hand to shake both Jude's and Lacey's hand. "I'm David Johnson. You came up from Lodgepole to check on us?"

"Yeah, it's something Lev feels needs to be done."

"Good ol' Lev. I think we're pretty well set."

Lacey noticed a truck still covered in snow. "You're able to drive out when the roads are clear?"

David turned toward his truck. "Yeah, there is a road on the other side of the property that leads into Garnet. That's where we get most of our supplies. Gonna be a few more days before the forest service plow makes it up this far. But we have a generator, lots of wood, stocked shelves and a greenhouse. I can get around on the snowmobile. We're ready for anything. I used to live in Seattle, worked as a financial guy. The stress was killing me, and I never got to see my kids." He cupped a hand on the teenager's shoulder. "Trying to teach them self-sufficiency."

"Dad, what about some aspirin for Winnie?" The teen pointed at Jude's backpack.

"Oh yes, if you have aspirin in that pack, we'd take that."

Jude slipped out of the pack and started rooting through it. He opened the first aid kit and pulled out two packets. "Probably only going to be three or four in each one. It's not a children's aspirin."

"We can cut it in half." Johnson took the packets. "Thanks. My wife likes to use herbal medicine, but sometimes you can't beat good old-fashioned aspirin. You folks are welcome to come in if you like. Wife said something about making a pecan pie."

Lacey glanced at Jude. They couldn't waste any time. "That sounds tempting, but we need to get going."

David offered them a tip of his hat. "Take care and say hi to Lev for me."

"You got it," Jude said. He turned to go but then turned back around. "Have you noticed any strange vehicles around here before the storm hit?"

David shook his head and then looked at his older son who also shook his head.

Jude still wasn't going to give up. "I don't suppose you've seen anyone headed up toward those two cabins that are above you or signs of someone camping out?"

Again, David shook his head. "One of the cabins is owned by some organization. The members can use it. The other is a vacation rental. Sometimes in the summer I run into people. If they are out here to hunt, they might come by and introduce themselves. But no one has made themselves known lately."

"Thank you," Jude said.

The younger boy and a girl about the same age emerged from the house. Lacey and Jude walked back toward the growth of trees with the sound of laughter and wood being chopped fading as they hurried along.

"They seem like a happy family," Lacey said. She hadn't meant for her voice to be tinged with sadness. "I suppose they exist in this world. Happy families. I used to think that I would get married and have kids, but now I don't know."

Jude stopped the galloping pace he'd been setting and turned to face her. "Yeah, I understand about life being derailed. I used to think I was going in that direction too, but then when I couldn't stop that murder-suicide." He shook his head. "I don't know... it's like I lost my way." He reached out and squeezed her arm, offering her a faint smile.

From the moment she'd met Jude, she'd been drawn to the bright dancing quality she saw in his eyes. The slightly upturned mouth that suggested a mischievous side. She felt so conflicted. She was attracted to him and had been right from the start, but he stirred something up inside her that made her want to run. They had only known each other a short time. Maybe she was drawn to him because they both had suffered great loss. But part of her wanted the past to remain buried.

An uncomfortable feeling, a tightening through her stomach, made her start walking again.

Jude kept pace with her. "Maybe if we talked about this. I don't know. Both of us had bad things happen. It sounds like we both gave up on a normal life because of it, marriage, kids, a home."

She walked even faster. "I don't know what there is to say. Talking about it just makes me hurt all over again." It felt like a rope was being wrapped tight around her chest.

Jude dropped back a few steps behind her. "Okay, I'll let it go."

She hurried through the trees toward the snowmobile. They came to where it was parked. Now things just felt tense and awkward between them.

"I'm sorry," she said.

Jude's attention was on the snowmobile.

"What's wrong?" she asked.

"Someone has been here." He pointed to a wet spot in the snow. "They punctured the gas tank." He leaned forward to have a closer look. "Could be a couple of bullets shot through it to make it leak out." He stood back up.

Both of them tilted their heads. Lacey listened as tension filled her body.

A rifle shot rang out. The sound bruised her eardrum. Jude pulled her to the ground, seeking cover behind the defunct snowmobile. Her belly pressed into the cold hard snow. Jude turned his head so he was facing her.

"Let's try to get back to the Johnsons'."

Lacey wasn't sure if that was a good idea. That might put the family in danger.

They jumped to their feet together and took

off running toward the trees. Another shot zinged through the air. And then another.

Jude grabbed her arm and pulled her toward a ditch surrounded by trees. He searched the forest. "Judging from the noise, whoever is shooting at us is really close." He pointed. "Shots came from over there. He's between us and the Johnsons' house. We can't get back to there."

"He'll stalk us through the forest." Her throat had gone tight with fear.

"We'll have to head the other way," Jude said. "Maybe we can work our way down to Mr. Wilson's house."

That was miles from here.

Neither of them moved.

"The Johnsons might hear the shots," she said.

"Maybe. It is hunting season. What if they don't think anything of it?" Jude continued to stare out, probably looking for the next place to take cover. She searched the trees where the shots had come from but saw no movement. Jude pointed back toward the snowmobile.

She nodded. They pushed up from the ground and ran back toward the snowmobile, diving behind it. The silence surrounded them. She lifted her head just above the seat of the snowmobile. At least when they were being shot at, she knew where the would-be killer was.

Jude tugged on her sleeve and they sprinted toward another cluster of trees. They ran for some time, making their way out close to the road though they stayed close to the forest to provide cover. Several times shots pinged off trees. They ran silently down the mountain.

The forest ended, giving them no choice but to dart out into the open. Lacey peered over her shoulder. The shooter was behind them. His muscular build and gray hair told her he was the first man they'd seen on the mountain. He lifted his rifle and aimed.

Her heart froze in her chest. She turned to face forward just as she felt herself falling through space. She'd come to a steep drop-off and fallen. She hit the ground and rolled head over heels. A mini avalanche followed in her wake sending a wave of snow behind her. She stopped rolling and landed in a sitting position with snow covering her legs.

Fortunately, her snow gear had kept her warm. Only her face was chilled. The field of white that surrounded her was blinding. She glanced above her, expecting to see the shooter taking aim. He hadn't made it to the edge yet.

She rose to her feet, not seeing Jude any-where. Had he fallen too or had he stopped fast enough to avoid the steep drop-off? She dare not call out to him. A hundred yards down the mountain was an outcropping of trees. She headed toward it. The softness of the snow had broken her fall. She wasn't bruised, only fatigued.

Where was Jude?

She had only run twenty paces when she noticed a dark object partially covered in snow. Heart racing, she ran toward it, fear-ing that Jude had been buried in the little av-alanche. As she drew closer, she saw that it was the backpack Jude had been carrying.

Terror warred with panic. Was Jude suffo-cated by the snow?

She leaned down. The backpack was not attached to a body. He must have fallen too and this had become detached as he rolled. She looked all around, not seeing Jude any-where. She slipped the backpack on.

Movement out of the corner of her eye drew her glance upward. The shooter had come to the edge of the cliff and was taking aim. He lifted the rifle.

She couldn't make it to the trees before he got a shot off. She dove to the ground and crawled through the field of white. A shot came very close to her. So close it must have lodged in the backpack.

A light breeze brushed the skin of her exposed face as she made her way toward the trees. Crawling solider style. Heart racing. Body tensed. Again, the silence surrounded her. She peered over her shoulder. The shooter fell partway down the cliff when some snow broke off. He'd dropped his rifle above him.

This was her chance to make a run for it while he climbed back up, got his rifle and lined up another shot.

She bolted toward the rocks and trees. Her boots pressed into the snow. She pumped her legs as her heart pounded. She fought for breath, running even harder, faster.

Like a baseball player sliding into home plate, she dove toward the cover of the evergreens. A bullet hit the tree in front of her. She hurried deeper into the trees. She peered out at the field of white.

Where was Jude?

Jude opened his eyes staring at the clear blue sky. He lay flat on his back. His head rested on a rock that protruded out of the snow. He must have been knocked unconscious. He remembered only the snow breaking beneath him, the ground giving way.

He'd been out so long, that despite the warm winter gear, he could feel a chill seeping into his skin. In his tumble, he'd lost a glove and the backpack. He unzipped his snowsuit and placed his frozen hand close to his chest to warm it. His gun was still there.

Jude pushed himself off the ground. When he heard what he thought were rifle shots, he lurched forward. The shots hadn't come anywhere near him. His heart squeezed tight. Lacey was in danger.

A line of trees blocked his view of where the shots must have come from. He ran toward them. Once on the other side of the trees, he was faced with an uphill climb. He must have rolled some distance in his fall.

He dug his feet in the side of the hill to get some traction, feeling a sense of urgency as another gunshot shattered the silence. He worked his way up the snowy hillside. As he came to the crest of the incline, he saw the shooter, the broad-shouldered man, standing on the edge of the steep drop-off that Jude must have rolled down. He followed the line where the rifle was aimed just in time to see Lacey disappear into the trees.

He saw now the furrows he must have created when he rolled down the hill. Other than that, a field of pristine snow lay before him.

In his fall he had rolled completely out of view of the shooter. In order to get to Lacey, he'd have to become a target himself.

Jude shrank back down the hill, running out of view for as long as he could. His cover ended. He took a breath and stepped out into the open. Dropping to the ground might make him harder to hit, but it would take forever to crawl across the white expanse to the trees where Lacey had disappeared. He opted instead to run fast and hard, moving in a zigzag pattern and dropping to the ground for short intervals so it would be hard to line up a shot on him.

His boots sank down in the snow as he hurried toward the safety of the trees. In his peripheral vision he saw the shooter step back, lift his rifle and take aim. Jude darted sideways just as another shot rang through the forest. Heart pounding, he kept his gaze on the edge of the trees. Another shot by his upper arm nearly knocked him over and took his breath away. He waited for the excruciating pain of a gunshot wound to disable him altogether, but the pain never came. It must have gone through the thickness of his snowsuit at the padded shoulder where it felt like he'd been punched hard.

Just as he reached the edge of the trees, he

glanced up. The shooter had backed away. But Jude had a feeling he'd merely gone back to his snowmobile so he could meet Lacey and him on the other side of the forest. Just because the shooter had opted not to tumble down the steep cliff where he and Lacey had fallen didn't mean the kidnapper had given up.

Jude entered the trees, his eyes searching. "Lacey." He sprinted. The canopy of branches meant that there was less snow beneath the trees. Still, he scanned the ground hoping to see her boot print. He kept running, shouting her name several more times.

Desperation filled his awareness. Where had she gone? She hadn't seen him. She probably thought she was on her own out here. The sound of the snowmobile grew louder. He kept on running, searching. Fear gripped his heart. What if the shooter caught up with Lacey before he did? What if she'd been shot before she got to the shelter of the trees? She might be lying somewhere bleeding, unable to respond to his cries. He pumped his legs, willing himself to go faster. He wasn't going to let anything bad happen to Lacey. Choosing a path that looked most like a trail, he wove through the trees, running for at least ten minutes.

She nearly crashed into him.

"I thought I'd lost you." Her hand rested on his chest. She tilted her head to look into his eyes. She was out of breath from running.

He gasped for air too as relief flooded through him. "I was afraid too." He touched her cheek with his ungloved hand, relishing the warmth of her skin and the radiance of the affection he saw in her eyes. The prospect of losing her had made him realize how much he cared about her. More than anything, he wanted to kiss her and to hold her close.

She studied him a moment longer and then cast her gaze downward, breaking the heat of the moment between them.

Snow started to twirl around them. Their clear blue sky had become overcast. In the distance, a snowmobile engine revved.

"He's still after us, isn't he?" Lacey took a step back away from him, turning a half circle in the forest, probably trying to come up with a plan of escape.

He was grateful to see that she had recovered the backpack of supplies. "You have the radio still?"

She padded her chest. "Yes, but we're not close enough to get a signal. I don't think. I lost my bearings when we rolled down that drop-off. Do you think we could get back to the Johnsons'?"

He wasn't exactly certain of their location either. "I think that we might end up even more lost. If the Johnsons heard the shots, maybe they'll come out and see the sabotaged snowmobile." He knew they shouldn't count on help coming for them. He stepped forward and squeezed her arm just above the elbow. The snowmobile grew louder. Though it made sense to try and find the road that lead back to town, it would make them too easy to track down. "We just have to go where that snowmobile can't go." He took several steps deeper into the trees, turning to look back at her. Her auburn hair had worked loose of whatever had fastened it into place, framing her face and making her brown eyes seem even more filled with light.

He had a flash of memory. She'd pulled away when that electric moment had passed between them a few minutes ago. She didn't want to talk about the tragedies that defined both their lives. The walls around her heart were just too high. He'd have to hold on to that warm wonderful memory of being with her in the café, knowing that that was all there would ever be for the two of them.

Why was he even thinking about that? They were lost. He turned back around, tracing a pathway through the trees with his eyes.

He wasn't quite sure where they were at in relation to the road. Maybe if they worked their way downward they would get to a place where they could radio for help.

Once they didn't come home in the evening, a search party might be sent out for them. Even if Lev or somebody else found the sabotaged snowmobile, it would take some tracking skills to figure where he and Lacey had ended up and by then it might be too late.

ELEVEN

Lacey stared at the back of Jude's head as she trudged a few paces behind him. They'd been walking for over two hours with no sign of any landmark to tell her where they were. What if they were moving away from the road? All she saw were trees, trees and more trees. The terrain had leveled off. The only good thing was they had not heard the snow-mobile for at least twenty minutes.

The tension between them was palpable. She'd looked into his eyes, and the affection there had frightened her.

She stopped, planting her feet. "I don't think we are making any progress here. We might actually be moving deeper into the for-est and getting more lost."

He turned to face her. His forehead wrin-kled. "What do you suggest?"

She picked up on the ire in his words. She suspected his irritation wasn't about where he was leading her. It was about her pulling away in the heat of the moment. She wanted to tell him that she had felt the electricity between them too, but it had made her afraid. Instead, she responded with an impatient suggestion. "I think we need to work our way back to the road so we can figure out where we are. I know it's not safe to just follow the road but knowing where it is would be the best way to navigate."

He tilted his head toward the sun in the sky, which was barely visible through the thickness of the trees. "You know he is still out there looking for us. He's not going to give up. Someone from town should come searching for us once we don't come in at sunset."

"But they won't know where to find us, Jude."

"I'm doing the best I can." Jude placed his hands on his hips.

Hearing the frustration in his voice made her soften. "I know you are. I'm sorry. I just don't think we could survive if we had to spend the night out here."

"Tell you what. Let's walk for another ten minutes or so and then head out toward the edge of the tree line to see if we can figure out where we are."

"Okay." She tilted her head to see where

the sun was. To the best of her recollection the road was east from where they were at. She pointed. "Probably the best choice would be to go that way."

Jude changed direction, instead of moving due north he cut across the forest in a more eastward direction.

He continued trudging through the trees, taking the path of least resistance since there was no clear trail. It had snowed off and on throughout the day, just a light snow that never turned into a full-on storm. If another snowstorm moved in, they for sure would not be able to survive the night outside. They had a few hours before it got dark.

They walked for several hours, stopped to eat and drink from the supplies in the backpack and then kept going. As the sun set low in the sky, she was giving up hope of ever coming out of the forest. It seemed to go on forever.

"Let's try the radio and see if we can get anything?"

He stopped and nodded.

She pulled the radio from inside her snowsuit and pressed the button that activated it. "Hello, is anybody out there? This is Snow Team One." She let up on the button and heard only static. She pressed the button again.

"Hello?" She spoke more slowly as a sense of hopelessness invaded her mind. "This is Snow Team One. We're in some trouble."

The silence on the other end of the line caused a tension to twist through her chest and stomach. She squeezed the radio a little tighter.

"Nobody is there, Lacey." Jude's words were soft and filled with despair.

She glanced in his direction. He turned away and crossed his arms over his chest. "We got a little more daylight left. Let's use it while we can."

Lacey put the radio back in her snowsuit and followed as Jude set an even faster pace through the trees. She stopped in a clearing that looked like a tornado had gone through—broken tree branches and muddy snow.

"What happened here?" Jude looked around.

She looked closer at the tracks on the ground. "Herd of elk went through here. See the tracks? When there is a bunch of them, they're like bulldozers."

"Where were they going?"

"Maybe looking for food. Maybe some hunters scared them."

It felt like the research that had brought her to Lodgepole in the first place was some faraway dream.

They continued to walk, still not finding an end to the forest or seeing any sort of landmark that might orient them. As darkness fell, the snow and the wind increased. She zipped her snowsuit up tighter. Jude placed his ungloved hand inside his snowsuit to keep it warm.

The sun slipped out of view, and the night grew cold. Wind blew snow in her face. She stumbled.

Jude turned around to look at her. "You okay?" He was carrying the backpack, which he took off. "I'll see if there is some kind of light or something in here. Maybe some flares. They'd be spotted now that it's dark."

He set the pack on the ground, leaning close to see. She kneeled as well as he turned over the objects that were in there. Food, water, medicine.

"There's a lighter in here." He held it up so she could see. "We could build a signal fire."

"What if it's spotted by the wrong person?"

"We could at least build a small fire to keep warm." Jude took one of the bandages out of the first aid kit and wrapped it around a stick, then poured the rubbing alcohol on it before lighting it to make a torch. "This will burn out after a while, but we can at least see a little better."

He handed her the torch to hold while he zipped the backpack up and slipped into the straps. Again, they took off at a steady pace. The landscape never seemed to change: evergreens, fallen logs, the occasional clearing with no sign of the road.

From time to time she heard a strange sound in the forest, some sort of wild animal maybe. She couldn't quite place the noise, not a bear or a mountain lion. At first it was faint and infrequent.

Jude must have heard it too. "A fox maybe? Whatever it is, it sounds like it's in pain."

"Foxes sound like crying babies when they're in pain. That's not a fox." Fear infused her words.

They kept moving. Jude's makeshift torch illuminated the ground in front of them. The path was wide enough for them to walk side by side. The strange noise died out altogether.

They walked for another twenty minutes. The sound from the animal returned, this time closer and more distinctive. Jude turned one way and then the other. The noise was clearly howling and yipping, a canine sound.

"Are there wolves around here?" Jude asked. The flame from the torch flickered on the side of his face.

A chill ran up her spine like a thousand tiny

spiders. "Yes. They're the primary predator of the elk."

"They move in packs though?"

"Usually unless they have been kicked out." Her throat was dry from fear. "Wolves aren't that noisy when they're hunting."

The barking was very close but still they couldn't see anything. She caught a flash of movement in the trees. "There." She grabbed the torch to aim it. Jude still held on to it.

She saw a flash of dark fur.

It was a canine and it did look like a wolf and now it was being quiet. Was it stalking them?

"What if it's a dog?" Jude stepped forward. "Hey buddy, come mere, puppy." He aimed the torch at sectors of the trees.

It could be a dog that had been abandoned because of the storm, left to fend for itself. "Mr. Wilson had dogs."

Jude whistled and called for the animal again. They heard yipping and then a black border collie with white markings emerged from the trees. The dog wagged its tail and jumped up and down.

Breathing a sigh of relief, Lacey knelt down and pet the dog who licked her face. The dog had tags. "This is Mr. Wilson's dog. It says his name is Bart."

"Maybe we're far enough down the mountain that his place is just around a corner."

"But why is this dog out running through the forest with another storm on the way?"

"I don't know. We must be close to Wilson's house. Maybe he'll lead us to it." Jude handed Lacey the torch and rummaged through the backpack for another long bandage. He tied it around Bart's collar. He petted the dog's ears. "Come on, boy, lead the way."

They took off. Bart put his nose to the ground running at first and then slowing down. Though he seemed content to stay with them and didn't mind the makeshift leash, his movement seemed random and erratic.

The wind blew, and the snow fell more intensely. Her face grew cold as they worked their way through the trees and across a clearing. The temperature was dropping.

The dog sniffed the ground from time to time but really didn't seem to be leading them anywhere. They were now headed downhill, but she wasn't holding out hope that they would find Mr. Wilson's house.

They kept walking. The torch died out, slowing their pace. Her nose and cheeks felt numb from the cold. Bart grew excited, barking and twirling in circles, jerking on the leash.

He might just be chasing the scent of raccoons or some other nocturnal creature. All the same, she kept pace with the excited dog.

The back of Mr. Wilson's house appeared first as shadows. There were no lights on at all. Though Bart continued to yip and pull on the leash, they slowed their pace.

Mr. Wilson had a rifle, and he was paranoid about being robbed.

As they approached the house, another dog came out of the shadows and greeted them. The old Lab was glad to see them and Bart. They circled around the house and knocked on the front door. No answer.

"Didn't he say he was staying in a back room because it was easier to heat?" she said.

The Lab disappeared around the side of the house. Jude untied Bart and let him go. "They must know how to get in. Let's follow."

She could barely make out Bart's dark fur against the blackness of night. The wind howled, and the snow had started to come down sideways. The dogs led them to a door that was ajar. The tiny room was more of a shed, maybe ten by ten feet and it was separate from the main house.

Jude knocked on the door. "Mr. Wilson?"

The dogs yipped and barked and wagged their tails. Jude tried the door. The knob turned.

"Mr. Wilson, it's the people from Lodge-pole. We checked on you yesterday."

The silence was eerie. Lacey tensed as Jude opened the door farther. The room was dark though she could make out the outline of a woodstove.

Despite the storm still raging, they searched all around the outside of the house and a little ways into the forest. She was shivering.

"We can't stay out here much longer," Lacey said. "Let's get warmed up and then we can look some more for Mr. Wilson."

They returned to the little room with the dogs trailing behind them.

They stepped inside. Jude touched the woodstove and opened the door on it. "Fire is out but the stove is still warm, so it went out recently." He grabbed some of the chopped wood stacked in the corner and lit the stove.

The dogs came inside and lay on the beds that had been set up for them in the corner. Lacey fumbled around until she found a lantern and lit it. When she shone the light around, she saw Mr. Wilson's rifle propped against the wall. Would he go anywhere without his rifle? She wondered too where the third dog was, the white one that looked like it was part pit bull. All of this was concerning.

With the stove blazing, Lacey reached her

hands out toward the warmth, shifting from foot to foot. Jude picked a blanket up that had been resting on a small nightstand. He stood beside her. His shoulder pressed against hers. "There's only one blanket. You can have it."

The fear she'd felt earlier was no longer there. There was something comforting about having him close. "We can share it."

He wrapped the blanket around his shoulder and then around hers. His hand brushed over her back. Jude had left the door on the woodstove open. Both of them stared at the crackling fire.

The dogs settled down on their beds. Bart whined before lying down.

"We're going to have to go looking for Mr. Wilson once we're warmed up."

"I know," she said. Now that they had a quiet moment, the memory of him looking into her eyes came back to her. There was a part of her that wanted him to kiss her. Her jaw tensed. Why did she feel so conflicted about this?

"Mr. Wilson wasn't a young man. Maybe he wandered away from the property and had a heart attack," Jude said. "He must have gone pretty far. We looked everywhere. Maybe he went to a friend's house."

"Maybe, but the door was left open. That's

why the dogs got out. That is the action of someone leaving in a hurry," she said. They'd worked together to get here. Over and over, Jude had shown her that he would protect her and not leave her. She wasn't sure what to say. "I'm sorry I didn't want to talk about losing my family."

Jude turned, grabbed another log from the stack and tossed it into the fire. "I understand. It's painful to open old wounds. I sure don't want to do it." He settled back down beside her.

Tears welled up in her eyes. "I guess I've been kind of closed down since the accident. I cut people out of my life who cared about me. I worked and moved around so I didn't have to think about it." The tears flowed. "I feel like I wasted the life God gave me. I don't want to do that anymore."

Jude took her in his arms and held her.

She sobbed, resting her face against the flannel of his shirt. His arms held her while she cried. She felt a release…anger, guilt and sadness that she'd been holding in for years. Finally, there were no more tears. She rested her face against his chest while his heart beat in her ear.

His fingers touched under her chin. She lifted her face to look into his eyes. He bent toward her and brushed his lips over hers. She drew closer, feeling the hunger of his kiss and wrapping her arms around his neck.

The blanket fell from her shoulders. She felt the warm smolder of attraction...and maybe something deeper. His arms held her as he kissed her again. When he finally pulled free, she felt light-headed but so alive.

It was as if she had spent the years since the accident in walking paralysis. Functioning but numb with pain.

He rested his forehead against hers and then kissed her cheek before shifting back. His hand found hers and he squeezed it tight.

She closed her eyes, enjoying the moment.

Jude's hand pulled away. She opened her eyes. Something in the corner of the room caught his attention. The look on his face was one of shock.

As she watched him rise to his feet, her mood shifted to fear. Jude picked up the object in the dark corner of the room. It was a small stuffed animal, a lamb. Holding the toy, he turned to face Lacey. "This was the toy Maria was holding when she was kidnapped."

TWELVE

Jude stared down at the toy he grasped in his hand. It felt as though his world had been flipped on its side and then turned upside down. Maria's mother said she always had the toy with her. The picture he'd been given of the child showed her holding it.

Lacey rose to her feet. "I'm sure there are a lot of stuffed toys like that around. Maybe Mr. Wilson has grandchildren or maybe the dogs play with it."

He shook his head. "It can't be a coincidence. Mr. Wilson must have been holding Maria here."

"Do you think he's in on the kidnapping?"

"It looks that way."

The dogs stirred from their beds, barking and flinging themselves at the door. Something had them excited.

Lacey moved toward the door. "I hear another dog barking."

While the dogs continued to bounce around, she and Jude got back into their boots. Jude grabbed a flashlight that rested on a chair. Lacey eased the door open only a slit so they could slip through but the dogs couldn't get out. Outside the wind was still blowing and the snow came down sideways.

The barking of the third dog grew louder as he emerged through the trees. The dog ran toward them, jumped in circles around them and then headed back toward the trees.

"He's trying to tell us something." Lacey hurried after the white dog.

Jude ran beside her, shining the flashlight. The conditions were not a whiteout. All the same, it was not a good idea to get too far away from the house.

As they ran following the dog, the intensity of the kiss they'd shared lingered in his memory. How quickly the mood had been destroyed by his discovery.

His feet pounded through the snow. Frustration rose up inside of him. When they'd checked on Mr. Wilson, he may have been only a short distance away from Maria and not have known it. Or maybe she'd been brought down here from the cabin. Though they still needed to search the property, he had the feeling Maria was not here any longer. Had Mr. Wilson taken her somewhere else?

The dog led them into the trees that surrounded Mr. Wilson's property. He stopped at what looked like a fallen log, sat back on his haunches and howled. Lacey and Jude sprinted toward the dog, arriving at the same time. Jude shone the light all around. The object that he thought was a log was not. The light washed over a body lying facedown. The white hair indicated that it was Mr. Wilson.

Lacey let out a sharp gasp and took a step back. She reached for Jude's arm. Jude stepped closer. The body was frozen but there were clear bloodstains on the back. "He was shot."

"So he wasn't involved?" Lacey's voice faltered.

Jude straightened his spine as his stomach twisted into a hard knot. "Mr. Wilson lived a very austere lifestyle. I'm sure a little cash would have persuaded him to watch a child."

"His conscience must have bothered him. So he was shot," Lacey said. "Maybe he threatened to tell the authorities."

"Or maybe that guy on the snowmobile just eliminates anyone who could turn him in. We need to search the rest of the property. I doubt Maria is still around. But there might be some clue as to where she's been taken. That car that I was chasing must be parked somewhere."

The dog whined and yipped and then paced. Something was upsetting him.

A bright light shone on the body and then on their faces. A man in silhouette stood not more than twenty yards from them.

Lacey's voice filled with panic. "He's come back for the body."

And now they'd been spotted. The dark figure advanced toward them. He was the same build as the man on the snowmobile, the broad-shouldered man.

"Run," Jude said.

Both of them sprinted toward the house. As he ran, he lost sight of Lacey. Several shots were fired. The proximity and power of the shots hurt his eardrum. He sprinted toward the house, shining the light in the trees. Without a flashlight, Lacey would be forced to move slower. He didn't see her anywhere. His heart squeezed tight with fear.

Another shot zinged by his head. Jude switched off the flashlight. It made him too easy of a target. The dog that had led them to the body continued to bark.

Without any light to guide him, Jude slowed his pace. He slipped from tree to tree.

The kidnapper was close enough that Jude could hear his footsteps. Light flashed into and out of the trees.

Jude pressed his back against the thick trunk of a tree. The kidnapper's steps crunched in the snow and landed on branches that crackled as they broke underneath his boots. Jude feared his raging heart and heavy breathing would give him away. He stood still as a rock. The kidnapper's flashlight continued to jump around.

He heard another set of footsteps moving rapidly. Lacey. Now the kidnapper turned his light toward where that sound had come from. Jude caught a flash of Lacey running and the kidnapper falling in behind her right at her heels. Jude could see the kidnapper's back as he raised the gun to take aim at Lacey. He had to stop him before he shot Lacey. There was no time to draw his gun. Jude ran toward the kidnapper, leaping on his back and taking him to the ground. The two men wrestled. The kidnapper hit Jude in the head. The blow stunned him as he lay on his back.

The other man had risen to his feet moving toward where he'd dropped his rifle. He'd lost the flashlight in the struggle, leaving them both in the darkness. Jude rolled away into the brush, pushed himself to his feet and fired a shot. It was too dark to see if he'd hit his target. Another shot whizzed by his arm.

He needed to find Lacey.

He sprinted toward the dark shadows of Mr. Wilson's house. He peered over his shoulder. The kidnapper must be looking around for his flashlight. It bought Jude a few precious seconds. His legs pumped as he neared the house. Where was Lacey? She might go back to the room where the dogs were to get that rifle. But she wouldn't stay there. There was only one way in and out. That would make her a sitting duck. And he didn't think she would run haphazardly into the forest either. There were piles of rubble and building materials and an old car on the back side of the property in addition to the car that was parked out front.

"Over here," came a whisper.

He heard Lacey's voice but had no idea where it had come from. Light flashed as the kidnapper appeared around the corner of the small shed. Jude dove toward a pile of rocks. The man stomped past him, shining the light everywhere.

It occurred to Jude that the man must have come on his snowmobile. Where had he parked it? If he could find Lacey and figure out where the snowmobile was, they could get back to Lodgepole. The kidnapper would be stranded. Wherever he had hidden that car, it wasn't going anywhere.

The kidnapper trudged back toward where Jude was hiding, swinging around his flashlight. Jude crouched lower as the man passed him.

The footsteps stopped. Jude could no longer see the light. He lifted his head, trying to figure out what had happened. The dog that was still outside had stopped barking. Silence fell around Jude like a shroud. He studied each sector of the yard looking for any indication of where the kidnapper may have gone.

Jude bolted up, still not seeing any movement. He turned.

A light flashed in his peripheral vision by the little shed. He crouched back down.

"I think you better come out wherever you are. I got your girlfriend here with a gun to her head."

The blood froze in Jude's veins.

From the loft where she was hiding in the main house, Lacey peered out. She couldn't believe what she was hearing. The kidnapper was trying to lure Jude out into the open with a lie. She watched in horror as Jude rose to his feet and stepped toward the little back room where the voice had come from. She had to warn him, but shouting would only alert the kidnapper to her position. She reached behind her and grabbed the first object that her hand touched, a metal mug. She tossed the mug close to Jude. It fell in front of him. He stuttered in his step then looked up. She waved, hoping he would see her in the dark. The attic space where she was hiding had a window-like opening but the glass had been replaced with plastic that she had torn away when she'd first cried out to Jude.

Jude studied the house, his head tilted up.

A shot reverberated through the winter cold. Jude ducked back down but then he took off running toward the front of the house. He'd seen her. She needed to meet him downstairs. She heard the door open just as she stepped on the top step that lead down to the main floor.

She hurried down the creaking steps, which were old and not stable. She could hear footsteps now in the other room. Though her heart pounded with excitement at seeing Jude, she dared not cry out. The kidnapper had no doubt seen which way Jude had run and was on his heels.

She was on the third to last stair when the board broke and her foot fell through. She tried to pull it up, but her boot was wedged in place. She was going to have to slip out of the boot and then reach through and get it.

Jude entered the room and ran over to her.

"I'm stuck. We don't have much time."

"Boy, am I glad to see you." His hand rested on her cheek and he gave her a quick kiss.

Even in the frenzy of needing to get away, the gesture melted her heart. She pulled her leg through without the boot.

From the other room, an intense banging sound filled the whole house.

"I locked the front door, but it's just a matter of minutes before he breaks it down or goes to the other door." Jude pointed at the back door, which was in the same room as the attic stairs.

There was no further banging at the front door in the living room. Was he waiting for them to burst through that door so he could shoot them, or was he running around to the back of the house to use the other door?

Lacey gripped Jude's arm. "We've got to go out through the attic window. It's the only safe option."

Jude nodded.

Lacey slid back into her boot, flipped around and climbed up the stairs. "These aren't real strong."

Jude was right behind her. "I see that."

They reached the floor of the attic just as they heard the back door swing open and bang against the wall. While they scrambled across the attic floor, she could hear the kidnapper stomp through the house. They had only minutes before he would check the front door and potential hiding places. Once he saw the stairs to the attic, he would probably figure out where they'd gone.

Lacey glanced around for something to use as a rope to lower down with. She had counted on being able to find something in the space that was stuffed with unwanted items.

The kidnapper's boots pounded on the wooden planks as he entered the kitchen and stopped. He was no doubt looking at the attic stairs.

Jude bent a foam mattress cover and shoved it through the window. "Come on, we're jumping."

There was no time to think. No time to argue. Jude disappeared in an instant and she was right behind him. She stuck her legs out the window and pushed off. She landed hard on her knees. The snow and the mattress cushioned the impact.

Jude grabbed her hand. "We have to find

his snowmobile or there is no way we'll be able to escape."

They ran toward the little shed. The third dog was waiting outside it, sitting and looking up expectantly. The dogs were warm in there and they had food. Jude stopped and opened the door so the third dog would be safe until help could come for them. His two compatriots greeted him with excited yipping and bouncing.

The move had cost them precious seconds. But it made Lacey admire Jude even more. They rounded the corner of the little shed just as another bullet whizzed past her. They ran into the forest. Without a flashlight, they couldn't see and were forced to slow down once they were in the trees.

Jude pointed. "He came from over there. We need to follow his tracks."

Lacey knew without looking that Mr. Wilson's body was off to the side. They moved as fast as they could in the darkness. She peered over her shoulder. The bobbing light behind her told her that the kidnapper had just entered the forest.

Jude chose a route. She stepped in behind him. When she glanced back, the bobbing light was no longer there. "Jude, I think he figured out we're trying to find the snowmobile and he's going to try to get to it first by swinging around that way."

Jude stopped and tilted his head, probably thinking or listening. He scanned the whole area around them. Though it was hard to make out much in the darkness, Lacey didn't see a snowmobile, only tracks that led out of the forest.

"Let's try to get there first." He glanced over his shoulder, then took off running. The steady rhythm of their footsteps crunching through the snow was all she heard.

There was no good choice here. They couldn't go back to the house and wait out the night. The kidnapper would come for them. Staying out in the elements without transportation wasn't a good idea either.

The forest ended, and they were faced with an uphill trek. They followed the tracks. The ground leveled off. They were on a sort of side road. She could see the tracks leading toward the forest and the parallel grooves that a snowmobile would make, as well.

She sprinted to keep up with him despite the deep snow. She could feel her leg muscles fatiguing.

The yellow-white glow of a headlight blared at them. Coming at full speed. The kidnapper had made it to the snowmobile before them. They ran to the side of the road and headed back downhill. She slipped and fell, rolling part of the way. The snowmobile came down the hill after them.

Jude found her and reached both hands out to pull her to safety. They ran. The snowmobile could only follow them as far as the edge of the forest. The trees grew too close together to get a snowmobile through.

Before they even got to the tree line, the snowmobile veered back up to the road. They entered the forest and slowed down.

She stopped to catch her breath. Her heart pounded wildly from fear and exertion. She could see Jude's breath as he sucked air in and out. He stood with his hands on his hips.

"Do you think he's going around to the other side to catch us when we come out?"

Jude shook his head. "Let's just keep moving. We should be able to hear him if he is close and still on that snowmobile."

"Thanks for saving me back there," she said.

He took her in a single-arm hug, squeezing her shoulder. "No problem."

They moved slower, walking single file. Lacey listened for the sound of a snowmobile motor. She thought she might have heard it behind them. She dismissed the noise as just being her imagination.

They stepped out of the forest. "I say we go to that room where the dogs are. It's warm and the rifle is there. If he hasn't gotten to it already. I have a few bullets left in my gun. One of us will have to stand guard at all times. If he comes through that door…"

Jude didn't complete his thought, but she knew what he meant. If the kidnapper wasn't already back on the property waiting for them, they could wait until daylight in the little room, but they'd have to shoot the kidnapper if he tried to get in. It wasn't a bad idea. The dogs could alert them to anyone approaching.

All the same, the thought of having to shoot another human being, even someone on the wrong side of the law, sent chills down her spine.

They approached Mr. Wilson's homestead with caution, moving from one place of cover to another looking for the kidnapper or his snowmobile.

THIRTEEN

Jude peered above the pile a snow. Lacey pressed close behind him. He could feel her breath on the back of his neck. Though much of it was covered in shadows, the little back room was within their view.

He couldn't see any movement anywhere, but their pursuer could still be lying in wait. He could have gotten back to the homestead way faster on the snowmobile than they could on foot. "Should we make a run for it?" They had one final sprint to get to the room where the dogs were.

"I'm with you." She patted his shoulder.

Jude burst to his feet, half expecting to be shot at. Lacey was right beside him. When he got to the door of the little room, the dogs barked on the other side. He touched the doorknob and pulled his pistol out. His heart squeezed tight. There was a chance the kidnapper was waiting inside for them.

Lacey stood off to one side. He did as well, turning the knob and pushing the door open. The dogs burst out, yapping and jumping on them.

Lacey laughed. "Someone is glad to see us."

Jude looked around the dark room searching the corners. The lantern must have gone out. "I think we are in the clear."

He stepped inside.

"I'll stay out here for a minute with the dogs so they can go potty."

Even that made his chest tight with fear. "Not too long in the open, Lacey."

He fumbled around until he found the lantern. The fire was still going, which provided some light when he opened the door. He relit the lantern and came to stand at the door with Lacey who was pressed close to the wall.

The dogs ran around sniffing all the new smells. Jude whistled and two of them came running. The third dog, the white dog who had been in the forest with Mr. Wilson's body, lagged behind.

They stepped inside, closing the door once the last dog had come in and settled on the beds with the other dogs. Jude turned the lantern on low. If the kidnapper did come back, he'd see the smoke from the woodstove and know that they were there. Maybe they should just let it die out. The room looked to be well insulated. They'd probably stay warm until daylight.

He put his own gun back in the shoulder holster. Jude stepped across the floor and grabbed the rifle, which was still propped in a corner. He checked to see that it was loaded. "I'll take the first watch." When he glanced over at Lacey, he read fear in her expression. "Why don't you try to get some sleep?"

She nodded and settled down by the fire, pulling a blanket over her body as she lay on her side. Jude chose a position opposite the door where if the kidnapper came through, he'd have a clean shot. The little room had two windows on opposite walls from the door. He'd have to watch those too.

He jumped up to see if he could lock the door from the inside. He could not. The toy that had belonged to Maria still sat in the corner of the room. His chest squeezed tight and he prayed that she was still alive. The prayer came easier this time. The roads weren't plowed yet, so the kidnapper could only move Maria somewhere else on the mountain or hide her in Lodgepole and she'd have to be transported via snowmobile. Maybe she had been in one of the empty cabins and moved here once the kidnapper feared they would be searched.

Lacey drew the blanket tighter around herself and tossed from one side to the other before growing still. Her breathing slowed. Bart, the border collie they had met in the forest, came and sat beside Jude. The dog licked Jude's cheek and then lay down close to his legs. It gave him some peace of mind to know that the dogs would alert if anyone drew close.

He watched the door for what felt like several hours. When he could no longer keep his eyes open, he woke Lacey so she could stand guard.

He handed her the rifle. "You know how to shoot one of these?"

"It's required for my job. Just in case I have to deal with aggressive wildlife." She took the rifle. He touched her cheek with the back of his hand. Her eyes were soft and welcoming, glowing with affection.

"I'll be okay," she said. "Get some sleep."

He lay down where she'd been and pulled the blanket over his body. It took him only a few minutes to fall asleep. He slept until light coming through one of the windows woke him.

He rolled over. The rifle was propped in the corner and Lacey was gone. Panic filled his awareness as he sat up and tossed the blanket to one side. He took in a breath. The dogs were gone too. Maybe she had just stepped outside to watch the dogs. He opened the door and glanced around. His chest felt tight again until he heard dogs barking.

Lacey came around the corner of the main house with the dogs trailing behind her. She held something in her hand. She smiled when she saw him. She ran toward him and held up two granola bars and an apple. "I found us something to eat at the main house."

His stomach rumbled at the sight of food. "Thanks." He looked around.

Both of them lifted their heads at the same time. Though it was faint they could hear the sound of a snowmobile engine. It could be someone from town searching for them or it could be the kidnapper coming back to look for them in the daylight.

"We better get out of here." At least now, he knew where they were in relation to the road.

They ran back to the little room, leaving the dogs inside but the door ajar so they could get out if they needed to. Once they got back to town…if they got back to town, they'd have to make sure someone came up to rescue the dogs. Jude grabbed his one glove and tossed Lacey hers. He stuffed the granola bar in his pocket.

They sprinted toward the trees. They were only a short distance into the forest when Jude saw why the kidnapper had given them a brief reprieve. Mr. Wilson's frozen body was no longer there. They had gotten maybe five hours' sleep total. That was how long it took to hide evidence like a body. He suspected that the kidnapper would continue his search until he killed both Jude and Lacey, thereby wiping out any chance that he would be caught.

The snowmobile motor noises stopped. Though he could not see through the trees, he had to assume that the kidnapper had come back to search the property for them since it was the most likely place for them to hide.

"They have got to be looking for us by now," Jude said. "Let's see if we can get to the road and be spotted before the kidnapper finds us."

The cold air chilled his face as they ran parallel to the side road that led to Mr. Wilson's property. Lacey kept pace with him. He pushed a tree branch out of the way and jumped over a log. Both of them were gasping for breath when they heard the snowmobile start up again. The trees had thinned enough that he could see the road up ahead.

They stepped out into the open. Behind

him he could hear the approaching snowmobile. They had a view of the road as it wound down the mountain. He glanced up the road where there were several sets of snowmobile tracks.

"What should we do?" He detected the fear in Lacey's voice as she gripped his arm.

His mind reeled. The unexpected. They needed to do the unexpected. "We're heading back toward the house through the trees, but we will loop around it and then up the mountain. The kidnapper is expecting us to head down the mountain toward the road. We're just going to have to trick him."

Their tracks in the snow would tell the tale to the kidnapper, but he would have to follow them on foot once he figured out they hadn't gone back to the house.

They were only a short distance back in the trees when they heard the sound of another snowmobile. Without a word, both of them turned and ran back toward the road. In the distance coming down the mountain was a different snowmobile.

Thank you, God.

They stood out in the road knowing that the kidnapper would stay hidden to avoid being caught. The snowmobiler stopped and flipped his visor up so they could see his face. "I'm from town. Lev sent me. We've all been looking for you."

"Boy, are we glad to see you." Without knowing why, Jude felt some hesitation.

"Hop on, it'll be a tight fit, but I'll take you back down the mountain." The driver flipped his helmet back down.

What were their options? None really. They could stay up here with the known kidnapper.

"We should go," Lacey said. Her voice held a pleading quality.

Lacey got on the snowmobile. He let go of his suspicions and squeezed in behind her. The snowmobile lurched forward.

He was glad to be headed back to safety and warmth, glad to be holding Lacey. Without a helmet his face got cold. He nuzzled in close to Lacey's neck. She patted his thigh.

His positive thoughts hiccuped. It seemed a little strange that the snowmobiler hadn't radioed the other searchers that he and Lacey had been found.

Tension threaded through Lacey's chest when the snowmobiler veered off the road that lead back to town. She pulled away from the driver's back where she'd been nuzzled in close to cut the wind on her face. Something was wrong.

She angled her head to try and see where they were going.

The driver took them up over a berm. The snowmobile caught air and landed hard, skidding to one side. All three of them fell off. Lacey rolled as a whirlwind of snow encased her. At least the landing was somewhat soft. Her face was chilled from the wind and she'd lost her hat in the fall. The flurry of snow died down and she saw Jude on all fours trying to get up. It appeared the driver had caused the accident on purpose.

The snowmobile engine was still running. The driver jumped to his feet and ran toward the snowmobile. He intended to leave them behind. She still wasn't fully able to figure out what was even going on. They were in a sort of bowl surrounded by forest above them.

Jude had gotten to his feet and was chasing after the driver of the snowmobile. Jude tackled him. They rolled around in the snow and then Jude pinned the man down. "What is going on here?"

Lacey pushed herself to her feet and ran toward where the two men were.

Still holding the man down by resting his knees on the other man's stomach, Jude nodded toward Lacey. "Take his helmet off."

Lacey kneeled down, took her gloves off

and reached to press the buttons that opened the helmet. She pulled it off. The man underneath the helmet had short blond hair. His eyes darted back and forth, filled with fear.

"What are you up to?"

"Please, I needed the money."

"What are you talking about?" Jude leaned closer to him.

Lacey stared at the man. His snowsuit had made him look bulkier than he actually was. Was it possible this was the tall thin man who had attacked her while they were in town? It wasn't the same snowmobile that had come at them. This snowmobile looked like one that was owned by the city. Of course, he wouldn't have come for them on a snowmobile he had tried to mow them down with.

"Someone paid you to try to kill us?"

The man looked like he might cry. "My wife has cancer. We had no way to pay for the treatment." The man coughed. "I can't breathe."

Jude took his knees off the man.

Still gasping, the man sat up.

"Somebody hired you? Who?"

The man stared at the ground and then lifted his head to talk. His eyes grew wide and then he fell over backward. A single bullet had pierced the middle of his forehead.

All the air left Lacey's lungs. As she stared at the dead man, her stomach churned. She feared she might throw up.

A numbness settled into her mind and body and everything felt like it was moving in slow motion. The snow by the man's head turned crimson. Jude grabbed her by the elbow and sprinted toward the snowmobile.

More shots were fired from above them at the rim of the bowl. Now she saw why they had been taken here. It made them easy targets. She suspected it was the broad-shouldered man shooting at them. He must have radioed the tall thin man to pick them up and bring them here to be shot. Now she understood what the phrase *shooting fish in a barrel* meant. The tall thin man was probably just supposed to leave them there. But when the shooter saw that he was talking to them, he'd been eliminated. Before they could even get on the snowmobile, shots hit it. The engine stopped running. Liquid, probably gasoline, leaked out onto the snow.

Jude slipped over the side of the snowmobile and crouched. She rolled off the seat and pressed in beside him. Her heart pounded. She still wasn't able to fully process what had happened.

How long were they safe here using the

snowmobile as cover before the shooter repositioned to have a clean shot at them? She surveyed the trees, catching some movement, a flash of white. The shooter must be in snow camouflage. "He's there. I think he went deeper into the trees."

"He must be moving to get another shot at us." Jude stared up at the untouched snow that led to the tree line. "We can't stay here. We have a few minutes while he repositions."

That plan would only work if he didn't come back out from the forest and see them running up the bowl to get to the trees. They'd have to run for some distance out in the open before they got to the trees that were on the opposite end of where they'd seen the shooter, even then they'd have to hope they didn't encounter him in the forest.

They took off, slowed by the depth of the snow. Lacey glanced nervously at the edge of the forest, seeing nothing. Though fatigued, she lifted her legs and kept going. They made it to the forest without being shot at again. Once at the safety of the trees, she stopped to catch her breath and listen. Bands of light streamed through the evergreens.

Jude tugged on her sleeve.

She was fully aware that they might encounter the kidnapper at any time. Their tracks in the pristine snow would reveal exactly where they had gone if the shooter slipped out to check their position. Maybe he had predicted which way they would run and was waiting for them. It wasn't like there were options.

A crackling sound somewhere deeper in the trees reached her ears. Her heart pounded. It could be human.

Jude put his finger up to his lips. He stepped carefully, and she followed. They moved slowly past one tree and then another. It was cold enough that she could see her breath.

She glanced around. Breath came out from behind one of the trees less than twenty feet away.

"Run." Her voice came out in a hoarse whisper. The rifle shot nearly drowned out her command. Her eardrum rattled from the percussive impact of the bullet breaking through the air.

Jude took off through the trees. She sprinted as well, running on a slightly different path. If they stayed close together, it would be that much easier to shoot them both.

She ran for several minutes, breathing heavily from the exertion. She'd lost sight of

Jude but could guess at where he was. The pathways through the trees were limited.

Another shot knocked a tree branch above her off. It hit her shoulder before falling to the ground. The trees seemed to go on forever. She wondered if she should move toward where the forest opened up to get an idea of where they were in relationship to the main road. That was their best hope for finding help.

Lacey glanced over her shoulder. Where had the shooter gone?

They ran as fast as the deep snow would allow. The snowmobile ride that had ended in the driver's death had gotten her completely turned around. The sun was in the middle of the sky, it was hard to get her bearings.

She hurried after Jude, glancing over her shoulder and wondering what had become of the man with the rifle. It had to be the same man who'd been after them all along, the broad-shouldered man who had run Jude off the road.

It was just a matter of time before he caught up with Jude and her.

FOURTEEN

Lacey fought for breath as she hurried down-hill after Jude through the trees. Jude seemed to know where he was going. Both of them continued to look over their shoulders.

After jogging for what felt like more than an hour, Jude slowed down. They hadn't seen or heard the shooter or the snowmobile.

They trudged, not talking. She was tired and hungry. She'd witnessed a man die right in front of her. "I need to rest." She slouched down using a tree trunk as a backrest.

Jude sat down beside her.

She wanted to cry but no tears came.

He wrapped his arms around her. "I know it's all been a bit much."

She lay her head on his shoulder. "That man who died in the bowl. It sounds like he did all this for the money for his wife."

They couldn't stay here. They had to keep moving. It got dark by five o'clock. That gave them some time. It felt good to rest and to be here with Jude even though their situation was not good.

Jude glanced at the sky again. "How far off the main road do you think that guy took us when we ended up in that bowl?"

"Not long. Maybe ten minutes before we got there." It was hard to even calculate. Walking was so much slower than going by snowmobile.

He squeezed her shoulder. "Lev and the others must be looking for us. They will widen their search when they don't find us on the main road."

Lev and the town of Lodgepole had limited resources and they were in a crisis situation. And the man who had shot at them in the bowl was still out there. "I'm sure they'll do all they can." She couldn't hide how hopeless she felt.

She turned to face him. He held her. She liked that he didn't tell her everything was going to be okay, because that wasn't necessarily so. He touched her ear and cheek with his palm. She closed her eyes relishing the warmth of his hand.

She let out a heavy breath and tilted her head toward him. He kissed her forehead and then her lips. He pulled back and gazed at her and then hugged her close. She let out a breath and relaxed.

He spoke into her ear. His voice barely above a whisper. "We have to keep moving."

"I know," she said. She pulled back and removed her glove so she could touch his jaw. "We should try to get to a high place, so we can try to see any landmarks that might help us figure out where we are."

He nodded. They rose together and headed uphill. The wind intensified as the temperature dropped and the sun slipped lower in the sky. They huddled close together as they walked until they came to a high spot that provided a view of the mountain below.

The sky had turned gray and it was hard to see much more than the outline of mountain formation and forest. Far off in the distance, the twinkling golden lights of Lodgepole were just barely visible.

She felt a mixture of relief and despair. "So far away," she said.

"But at least we have an idea of where we're at."

The cold made her face feel numb and her stomach growled. She turned in a half circle, hoping to see some lights that indicated a house or cabin close by. They could head toward the lights, but at some point, they'd descend into a valley and the mountain in front of them would block their view of Lodgepole. In a few more hours they would be in total darkness. She saw no sign of the mountain road that led into town.

She turned toward him. "I'm not sure what to do."

"Let's hike a little farther up and see if we can spot anything else." He offered her a comforting smile.

She knew that Jude had made the best decision in a terrible situation. They could not stay out here all night. They'd freeze to death. She knew also from having worked outside in the winter that every step they took expended precious energy.

They trudged a little farther up the mountain through a grove of aspens. Though there were no leaves left on the trees, their white trunks glowed in the darkness. They came to another vantage point and peered out. The lights of the town were still visible.

Far below them, she saw a moving light. "That has to be where the road is." At this distance there was no way of knowing if the snowmobile belonged to a searcher or to the man who had tried to kill them.

Jude squeezed her arm. "That's where we go, then."

They headed down the steep incline. She angled her foot and dug her heels into the snow to create a secure foothold. The snow seemed to be cascading around them. She was aware that this high up, with as much snow as there had been, the avalanche danger was significant.

The snowmobile headlights disappeared from view probably rounding a corner on the mountain road. In the nighttime silence, the hum of the snowmobile motor echoed up the mountain.

They headed downward in a straight line. Several times they encountered snowmobile tracks that weren't on the road. People had been all over the mountain, maybe searching for Jude and Lacey. Once they were down in the valley, they could no longer see the lights of the town. They trekked back up the mountain. Fatigue had settled into Lacey's leg muscles. She couldn't stop thinking about sleep and food. Several times her eyes bobbed shut and then she jerked awake as she walked. The important thing was to keep moving. The sound of the snowmobile faded.

Finally, they stepped out onto the road. The lights of Lodgepole were again visible but still very far away. Jude reached over with his gloved hand and squeezed hers. He'd stuck the hand that didn't have a glove into his pocket.

"We should pray," she said. Why did things have to get to this point before she even thought to reach out for the help that was always there, always available?

They walked side by side. "God, we are afraid and cold," Jude said. He took several more steps without saying anything.

"We know that You are the God who can do anything," she said and then she fell quiet. Her breath came out in cloud-like puffs. She listened to their muffled footsteps on the soft snow. The fabric of their snowsuits made a swishing sound as they moved along the road.

Jude picked up the prayer, asking God to give them the strength to keep going. And then he recited the first lines of Psalm 23. "The Lord is my shepherd. I shall not want."

She said the next line.

And so they walked reciting the psalm that offered so much comfort and promise of God's care. Each of them saying a line and then walking in silence for several seconds before the other voiced the next part of the psalm.

Once they were finished, they trudged without talking until Jude cleared his throat.

"I owe you a debt of gratitude for restoring my faith."

"I didn't know that's what I did."

The wind blew snow around. The stars twinkling above them offered only a little light to see by. In spite of the bleakness and the cold, she felt her hope renewed.

Jude stopped for a moment and lifted his head. "I think I hear something."

She couldn't hear anything but the wind rushing through the treetops of the evergreens that grew close to the road. The odd mixture of joy and then dread flooded through her. Was the snowmobile they heard coming to rescue them or kill them?

Jude's mind shifted into high gear. He tuned his ears to his surroundings trying to detect if the snowmobile he heard was above them or below them. He was keenly aware that his feet and face felt numb. His legs weighed a thousand pounds. He was beyond exhausted.

The sound faded rather than grew closer but the echo effect of the mountain made him uncertain if he was hearing correctly. The only thing he knew for sure was that there was a snowmobile somewhere close.

Then the sound faded. He listened, thinking maybe he would hear it again. His hope deflated like a balloon losing air. An intense gust of air hit them. He turned slightly and put his gloved hand up to his face to protect it.

The wind died down. He peered out. First at the lights of Lodgepole and then down the mountain. A lump in the snow several turns down the mountain road caught his attention. He walked to the edge of the road squinting to make sure he was seeing clearly. His spirits lifted. "I know where we are."

She stepped toward him and he pointed down to where the lump was. She followed the direction of his hand. "Your wrecked car." Enough of the snow had blown away to make the top part of the car visible.

"We must be close enough to radio the base station."

Lacey touched her chest, her voice filled with pain. "I took the radio out of my suit when I slept in Mr. Wilson's little shed. I forgot to grab it in all the excitement. I can't believe I did that."

"Don't beat yourself up," Jude said. "We'll figure this out together. The car will provide some shelter for us."

They cut off from the road and moved in a straight line toward the half-exposed car. Once they got to it, it was clear the front doors were too buried in snow to open. They dug away at a back door with their hands. He stuck his ungloved hand in his pocket to warm it and kept digging one-handed.

Out of breath from the frenzy of digging, Lacey stood back. Jude reached for the door handle, stepping aside so Lacey could get in first. He crawled in after her.

The entire front windshield was covered in snow. They both sat trying to catch their breaths.

"Do you have, like, a winter survival kit in here?" Lacey slumped against the seat.

He thought for a moment. The morning he'd taken off to tail the car the kidnapper had stolen felt like an eon ago. He shook his head. And then he turned to the cargo area in the back where he had a blanket for his dog. He handed it to her.

"What about in the front seat? Any food or anything that might be useful? I'm smaller. I can crawl through and look."

Again, he searched his memory. "There's a flashlight in the glove compartment."

She crawled over the front seat, opened the glove compartment and handed him the flashlight which he shone so she could see better. She opened the console that was in between seats and laughed. "Ketchup packets. A couple of sugar packets."

Jude rubbed his hands together. "We will dine in style."

She let out a little laugh before shoving the packets into her pocket. "Food is energy at this point." She searched around a little more before joining him again in the backseat. "Maybe save it for when we hike out."

They both got underneath the blanket for warmth. He wrapped an arm around her. She rested her head on his chest. "God is funny, isn't He?"

"What do you mean?"

"We prayed thinking the answer to our prayers would be for one of the snowmobilers to find us."

"But God saw another option." He nestled close to her. They'd be able to stay warm enough until daylight. "I'll take first watch." The man with the rifle was probably still searching for them. He listened to the steady soft sound of Lacey's breathing as she slept. He turned his head slightly to stare out at the darkness.

His eyelids felt heavy. He nodded off and shook himself awake. Outside it was still dark. Lacey stirred awake. She pulled away from him.

"I feel more rested. I'll sit watch, so you can get some sleep," she said.

He was grateful for her offer. He leaned his head back and closed his eyes. His brain fogged from exhaustion and he felt himself relaxing as he fell into a deeper sleep.

He awoke one time in the night. Lacey had moved away from him and was resting her cheek against the door. He saw no lights outside. When he rolled down the window in the backseat all he heard was the wind. He had only a view out the back window where he saw no snowmobile lights.

He fell back asleep, waking when the sun shot through the window and warmed him. Lacey was already awake.

She touched her stomach. "Boy am I hungry." She drew out the sugar and ketchup packets and divided them evenly. They ate quickly. Jude pushed open the door they had dug out of the snow.

They ran straight down the mountain, connecting with the road as it wound toward Lodgepole. They'd only gone a short distance when they heard a snowmobile above them.

Jude glanced up.

"I saw him," Lacey said. "He has a rifle with him. He must have been waiting for us. I wonder why he stayed away all night."

Her words sent a bolt of fear through him. He looked around for a hiding place as the sound of the snowmobile grew louder.

FIFTEEN

As they hurried toward a snowdrift that would provide some cover, Lacey pushed aside the panic that filled her. They slipped behind the drift, pressing close together.

If the man with the rifle stopped to look over the edge of the road, they would be spotted, their brightly colored snowsuits easy enough to see in a field of white. If he kept going down the road, there was a chance he would whiz past them.

Heart racing, she bent forward hoping no part of her showed above the drift. Jude faced her, crouching low, as well. He stared into her eyes. Neither of them dared make a sound. Though her legs were starting to cramp in the tight position, she remained still. They listened to the snowmobile *putt putt* along. The guy must be looking all around to be going that slowly.

The motor was the loudest as it passed by them on the road.

She stared into Jude's eyes. Just a few more minutes and they would be in the clear as long as he kept heading down the mountain. She raised her head getting a glance at the back end of the snowmobile before it disappeared. Her breath caught. There was a second smaller passenger on the snowmobile. Maria.

"He has her! He has the little girl. That's why he didn't come after us last night."

Jude's eyes grew wide and round. "The roads must be open. He's taking her out of here." Standing, he reached in his snowsuit for his gun, but thought better of it. He couldn't risk hitting Maria. "We have to stop him."

He jerked his head to one side. Before she even had time to look up the mountain to whatever had alarmed him, a thundering roar surrounded her.

Avalanche!

All that snow and then days of it warming up a little had caused them to be in the wrong place at the wrong time.

They bolted and headed downhill trying to outrun the wave of snow. She felt her body being picked up and tossed around. She saw flashes of color. Jude's snowsuit. She landed on her bottom. The snow cascaded around her, enveloping her. She had a terrifying moment of not being able to breathe. The wall of snow moved past her and then she felt herself thrust upward. Though she was covered in snow from head to toe, she was upright. She wheezed in a shaky breath.

A pile of boulders in front of her had created a sort of pocket where the snow had gone around her. Her stomach and her cheek were pressed close to one of the rocks. Lacey stood up brushing the snow off her face and sleeves. She traced the pathway of the snow which now blocked part of the road. She'd been right on the edge of the avalanche. Frantic, she looked around for Jude. All she saw was a field of white.

With some effort she climbed up on the rocks and looked all around. She prayed that Jude was not buried. It would be only minutes before he suffocated. Whiteness everywhere. The kidnapper hadn't gone that far down the road before the avalanche hit. She saw his taillight far away down the road. He was getting away and he had Maria with him.

Her priority was finding Jude.

She saw some thirty feet from her a spot of pink in the white field. It was a hand. The depth of the snow slowed her down as she raced toward where Jude was. As she drew closer, she deduced that the force of the avalanche had ripped his boot off. His pink foot stuck out, as well. She sank deep into the snow. Pulling her leg up, she took as big a stride as she could. Each step was laborious. By the time she reached Jude, she was out of breath. She dug furiously where she thought his head might be. She saw curly hair and then a forehead.

"Jude?"

He didn't open his eyes or move. His lashes were white with snow. His face red and lifeless from the cold. Her emotions plummeted to the depths of despair as she pulled off a glove and reached a hand out to touch his cheek.

He wheezed in a breath, and his eyes shot open. He stared at her as though not comprehending who she was.

"Jude." Her voice filled with elation. "Let's get you dug out of here."

She freed both his hands first and then his upper body so he could help dig out his lower half. His body had twisted at an odd angle and she feared something was broken and he just wasn't feeling the pain of the injury because he was numb from the cold. She scraped the snow away from the leg that no longer had a boot.

She stood back and reached for his hands to pull him up. "Is anything broken?"

Jude still had a dazed look on his face. He shook his head slowly.

He was shivering. She unzipped her snow-suit and slipped out of the top part of it. She was dressed in layers. She pulled her sweater off leaving only a T-shirt. She pointed for him to sit back down and wrapped the sweater around his bare foot. The makeshift boot was awkward, but the wool would wick some of the moisture away at least.

He was probably weak from being buried alive. "Can you walk?"

He nodded. She reached a hand out to help him get to his feet again.

They walked a short distance. When they were free of the deep snow the avalanche had brought down, he stopped and leaned against a tree.

He reached out and touched her face. "Thanks for digging me out."

His hand was cold on her cheek. "I'm just glad I found you in time," she said.

His expression changed. His jaw hardened, and he drew his eyebrows together. The light still had not come back into his eyes. "I almost died back there…just like you in the freezer."

She leaned toward him. "It's not like your whole life passes before you, but you do have a moment of wondering if you made the right choices."

"Yeah, exactly." Jude seemed to be very far away in his thoughts.

She touched his face. "We have to keep moving. I'm afraid you're going to end up with frostbite."

"Yes, we have to get to town. Alert the authorities about the kidnapper having Maria. I doubt he's headed to Lodgepole. We can't catch him now." He touched his side. "It hurts when I breathe. I wonder if I broke a rib or something."

Though progress was slow, they found a path where the snow was smashed down, probably by deer, outside the perimeter where the snow had cascaded down the mountain.

They walked for at least a half hour before Jude needed to rest against a tree.

She heard a tremendous roar. She left Jude and stepped out into the clear where she had a view of the road down below. It took several minutes before she saw four snowmobiles headed up the mountain. They must have seen the avalanche from town and come up to assess the damage. She hurried back to get Jude.

Jude still sat slumped by the tree. His eyes had life in them again. She sat down on the ground, as well. Her heart pounded. They needed to get out to the road to be spotted by the snowmobilers.

Knowing that the avalanche risk was still high and could be triggered by the noise of so many snowmobiles would the men even come up this far? She caught a flash of movement through the trees. Several deer stepped out into the open, tails flicking nervously as they looked around and then took off running. The avalanche had stirred them up.

It sounded like the snowmobiles were still headed up the mountain.

She tuned in to the sounds around her. Her heartbeat drummed in her ears. She tensed, drawing her lips into a tight line. She prayed another avalanche would not be triggered by the snowmobiles.

Because of the echo effect, it was hard to tell exactly how close the snowmobiles were. Jude leaned forward. From where he was sitting, he must have a view of the road. He motioned for her to get up.

They ran through the trees and out to the road. Two snowmobiles were a hundred yards away but headed toward them. The others must have remained behind. Lacey thought she might collapse from relief. She peered over her shoulder just as the deer disappeared back into the forest.

The men stopped. One of them was Lev. He pulled his helmet off. "Boy, are we glad to see you. Thought for sure you were goners. Is the road blocked off farther up?"

Jude nodded.

Lev glanced down at Jude's foot wrapped in her sweater. "You two probably need to be looked at. Get on and we'll take you back to town."

Jude pointed down the road. "The man who took Maria is escaping with her. He'll have an hour head start on us."

"The roads are just now opening up. I can make some calls to have law enforcement be on the lookout for a man with a little girl."

"Okay, but nothing that draws attention. The kidnapper threatened if law enforcement was involved something bad might happen to Maria," said Jude.

"Can do." Lev's voice filled with compassion. "Let's get you to a place that is safe and warm. We've got another man missing."

Lacey opened her mouth to explain that the

missing man was dead, but she was experiencing a sort of shock now that they were safe.

"Is the man tall and thin with short blond hair?" His voice as well sounded weak.

"Yes, his name is Dale. He volunteered to go out and look for you two," said Lev.

"He's dead. The man who has Maria shot him," Jude said.

Lev stared at him for a moment. He lowered his voice. "I didn't know Dale. He kind of kept to himself. He was new around here."

Jude's voice was solemn. "He said his wife had cancer."

Lev nodded. "I heard that too." Lev let out a heavy breath. "Sounds like you have quite a story to tell the sheriff over in Garnet. My priority has to be your safety."

Jude stood for a long moment. His jaw set tight. But then, he nodded. Maybe accepting Lev's plan.

Jude took Lacey's hand and led her toward the second snowmobiler. She got on and he patted her back. The gesture of care touched her. He walked with some effort over to Lev's snowmobile and got on. He looked like he was about to fall over from exhaustion.

The trip down the mountain went by in a blur. At some point the two other snowmobilers joined them.

Lacey felt herself nodding off as the edge of Lodgepole came into view. She had a vague awareness that the snowmobile had stopped. A moment later, someone picked her up and carried her. She opened her eyes briefly to see Jude's soft smile. He was clearly as worn-out as she was, not only from lack of sleep but from all the trauma.

She felt herself being placed somewhere soft and a blanket was put over her. Jude's voice sounded very far away as she heard him saying he needed to talk to the sheriff.

She recognized Nancy's voice telling him he needed to be looked at by a medical professional. Her sleep felt more like she was passing out.

She awoke when the growling of her stomach overwhelmed her need to rest. She sat up. She was alone in Nancy and Lev's living room asleep on the couch. The curtains were drawn and the lights were out. Hushed voices came from another room.

She rose to her feet and entered the kitchen where Jude and Nancy were sitting at the kitchen table. Jude rested his hand on a cell phone that he must have borrowed. An empty bowl sat beside him.

Nancy smiled. "I'm sure you're hungry. Have a seat."

Lacey nodded and sat down beside Jude. He had dark circles under his eyes and his skin looked sallow. "Did you get a doctor to look at you, Jude?"

"Later. We've got things to take care of. I've been on the phone to the sheriff over in Garnet."

Nancy sat a bowl of soup down in front of Lacey. She pushed some crackers that were on the table toward her.

"Jude's foot looks like it has some frost-bite," Nancy said. "His ribs are bruised too. I tried to tell him that getting over to the sheriff could wait a few hours. The sheriff has put out an all-points bulletin for the kidnapper and the little girl."

"I need to talk to the sheriff in person. I want to help with the search for Maria," Jude said. "I haven't been able to get hold of George yet. He's not picking up."

Lacey spooned up the soup. The warm liquid soothed her empty stomach.

"Lacey, would you be willing to go with me since you can identify the kidnapper? I gave the sheriff a basic description over the phone based on what you told me. But can you look at mug shots so we can put a name with the face?"

Lacey nodded. If she still felt tired after a short rest, Jude must be beyond exhausted.

"It's an hour drive to get to Garnet," Nancy said. "Why don't you at least let Lacey drive so you can sleep?"

"That would work." Jude turned toward Lacey. "Nancy is loaning us her SUV. We need to hurry."

"I'll finish my soup so we can go."

"I'll go warm the car up for you." Nancy rose to her feet. "And, Jude, grab a pair of Lev's boots from the closet by the door. He has big feet, so your feet might be swimming in them but at least you'll have boots. I'll get some extra pairs of socks." Nancy left the room.

Lacey heard the outside door open and close.

She finished her soup. The meal had strengthened her. Ten minutes later, she was behind the wheel of Nancy's SUV. Jude crawled in the back along with a blanket Nancy had given him.

Lacey backed out of the driveway. "I know you have a lot on your mind, Jude, but Nancy is right about rest."

"I know," Jude said. "But I don't want this guy to get away with that kid. Who knows what he has planned?"

She rolled up the street toward the edge

of town. Would the man with the rifle hide Maria somewhere and come after them? She checked her rearview mirror as she came to the city limits and pulled out on the two-lane road that led to Garnet.

Damage from the snowstorm was still evident. Snow was piled high on either side of the road and there were cars covered in snow that must have slid off. She prayed that the people in the accidents had made it to safety.

"I talked to Lev while you slept. The man who was shot in the bowl was from Lodgepole and his wife was in a hospital in Denver. Lev said Dale was antisocial and not mentally stable. He lived in a run-down old Victorian on a big lot. Lots of junky cars in the front yard. Kept to himself."

"I remember walking by that house when we were searching." And she remembered seeing the dark-haired man standing by the window who had slipped out of view. Maybe he was Dale's paranoid brother. "Did he live alone?"

"I don't know. I didn't ask. Why?"

"There was someone else in that house, a dark-haired man."

"A friend maybe?" Jude's voice grew weaker as exhaustion had set in.

She drove for another five minutes passing only fields with drifted snow.

She looked down at the gas gauge. She should have thought to fill the tank before leaving town. Conditions were still not perfect. She drove slowly. Several cars passed her. An equally cautious driver in a black van eased by her. A sign indicated that a gas station was up ahead.

She pulled in. When she peered over her shoulder, Jude was fast asleep. She filled the gas tank up. She had only cash, so she went inside to pay. The clerk was a lanky teenage boy who leaned over the counter flipping through a magazine. She handed him the cash and waited while he made change.

A news program on a television, mounted to the wall, droned in the background as the kid counted out her change and excused himself. He exited out the side door. He had smelled of smoke so maybe he was out having a cigarette.

Her eyes were drawn to the television set as a breaking local news story flashed on the screen. Her breath caught and she looked around for the remote control to turn up the volume. She found it behind the counter. She pressed the volume button.

She couldn't believe what she was seeing.

The news story was about how Maria Ignatius had been returned safe and sound to her parents in a Montana town. A news story that should have made her happy. Should have made her want to run out to Jude and shake him awake so he could hear the good news.

As she stood alone in the gas station though, she knew something was terribly wrong. On the screen flashed a scene of little Maria with her father, George. Lacey felt like an elephant had just sat on her chest. George was the man she'd seen at the window of the Victorian house where Dale lived. George had been in Lodgepole at the time of his daughter's kidnapping, and he knew Dale.

He had led Jude to believe the calls were coming from out of state. Was it possible that George was somehow connected to his own daughter's kidnapping? Why?

Lacey hurried outside to tell Jude. She swung open the back door of the SUV. Jude wasn't there.

A hand went over her mouth.

A gruff voice spoke into her ear. "Where's your boyfriend?"

She shook her head.

"Fine, we'll just use you as bait."

The scenery whirred around her as she

was dragged across the icy gravel lot. A door clicked open and she was shoved into the back of a van. She caught a glimpse of her kidnapper just before he slammed the door. The black van must have followed them from Lodgepole or just outside of it. She recognized the man as the one who had hunted her and Jude from the beginning on the mountain, the gray-haired muscular man. He must have turned Maria over to somebody who did the exchange giving him time to come after Lacey and Jude. The van smelled like grease. Her hand touched dirty carpet.

She wasn't tied up. She could still get away. She lurched for the side door that had just been opened. Her hand reached for the door handle. She slid it open.

Jude was just coming around the side of the building. A look of horror spread across his face.

A man shoved her back in and slammed the door. She caught sight of Jude running toward the van.

The front door opened and shut. The motor of the van roared to life.

She heard a fist pounding on metal and Jude shouting her name as the van gained speed. Would the information that George

Ignatius was somehow connected to his own daughter's kidnapping die with her? Lacey collapsed on the dirty carpet.

SIXTEEN

As he raced toward Nancy's car, Jude had the sensation of being punched in the stomach and hit in the head at the same time. He jumped into the cab and turned the key in the ignition. He'd awakened to find the car stopped and assumed Lacey was inside paying for the gas. He'd noticed the bathroom on the side of the building and gotten out of the car to use it.

He used the restroom and then wandered around the back to stretch his legs where he found a teenage boy sitting on milk crates staring at his phone. He'd exchanged a hello with the kid and then gone to get back in the car. In those brief minutes, Broad Shoulders had had time to grab Lacey. The van may have already been parked there. He wasn't sure. He was still groggy from his deep sleep and not as observant as he should have been.

He pressed the gas and sped up after the

van. Jude was able to stay close to the van as it sped down the highway. He pulled the phone Nancy had loaned him from his pocket. If he drew his concentration away from the road, it meant slowing down to call the sheriff. He pressed the button on the phone and put it on speaker, informing the deputy who answered as to what was going on.

The distance between himself and the van increased. He ended the call and pressed the gas. He drew close to the van and then increased his speed to come alongside it and maybe run it off the road. An oncoming car made him slip back behind the van again. He stayed close to the van's bumper looking for his chance when the van turned suddenly onto a side road without signaling. Jude took the turn to follow at a tight angle, sliding sideways. This road was paved and plowed but still icy. The piles of snow on either side of it made it into almost a one-lane road. There was no way to run the van off the road. He could only tail it and wait for the road to widen. Several times, he tried to ram the van from behind to make him go into a snowbank, but he only managed to tap the bumper before the van gained speed.

They passed a house with several barns and outbuildings and then the landscape flattened out. Though the fields were covered in snow, they were probably used for planting in the spring.

Jude continued to follow the van. The driver maintained the same distance between them. Clearly this was some sort of trap to get both of them to a vulnerable and isolated place. All the same, he could not abandon Lacey. He had to find a way to free her.

He slowed and tried the phone again. The sheriff would be looking for him on the main road. Before he could press the call icon, the phone slipped out of his hand and fell on the floor of the passenger side.

Jude gripped the wheel and maintained his pace. They drove for what seemed like at least twenty minutes. In all that time, the only living things they encountered were a field of sheep. The road turned from paved to gravel.

He began to wonder what the guy in the van had in mind when he pulled over on a shoulder, the first one they'd encountered.

Jude hung back on the road waiting to see what the man was going to do. His gun was still in his shoulder holster which was in the backseat. He'd taken it off when he'd lain down to sleep. Jude turned to try and reach it. His fingers were inches from it.

He glanced back. Broad Shoulders had gotten out of the van and was opening the side door. What had the man done with Maria? He'd had over a two-hour lead on them. Maybe she was in the van with Lacey? Broad Shoulders reached in and grabbed Lacey, yanking her toward the road as he drew out a gun and pointed it at Lacey's head.

Jude had the awful feeling that neither one of them was going to get out of here alive. Both of them could identify this man. Though the evidence against him for being connected to the kidnapping was circumstantial, he had probably killed Mr. Wilson and Dale. He had repeatedly tried to kill Jude and Lacey.

No, his intention was clear. He was going to shoot both of them.

The man nodded his head, indicating that Jude needed to get out of the cab of the SUV. Jude glanced back at his gun.

With Lacey in tow, holding her by her ponytail and pressing the gun to her temple, the man marched toward the car. Lacey's expression was filled with anguish. And then he saw her close her eyes and her features softened.

She was praying.

He needed to do the same.

He pushed open the door even as the words tumbled through his head.

God, help me find a way to get Lacey free and us to a safe place.

He stepped out and put his arms up in the air.

Broad Shoulders pointed the gun at him. "Open your coat. I need to see that you're not armed."

Jude held his coat open.

"Turn around," the man commanded. "Lift your coat up."

Jude did as he was told and then turned to face the man. Satisfied, the man put the gun back on Lacey's temple.

His teeth showed when he grinned. "So which one of you wants to die first?"

God, please.

Broad Shoulders grimaced. The rage Jude saw in those eyes was scary.

Jude's gaze moved upward for just a second as relief spread through him. The man was standing almost underneath a tree whose branches were heavy with snow. One of the lower branches had a chunk of snow that looked like it might slip off at any second.

"Please, there must be something we can work out between us." Jude kept his hands in the air but took a step toward the man, knowing that it would make the man take a step back. One more step and the man would be right underneath the branch. He needed to buy some time.

"There is nothing to work out. I'm not going to jail," the man said.

"Do you think they're not going to find any evidence that links you to those two dead men on the mountain? Let alone the kidnapping of Maria Ignatius."

The man raised his eyebrows in a quick spasm. Again, it wasn't solid evidence but what Jude read in that expression was guilt.

"I have a way to get out of the country so fast, I'll be somewhere they can't find me before they even bring the body bags in…if they ever find them."

Fear shot through Jude. "What have you done with Maria?"

Something flashed across Lacey's features and then was gone. She shook her head. A movement so slight that only he would notice it as he faced her. She knew something about Maria.

Without moving his head, Jude gazed upward. The snow was hanging, ready to slip. He just needed the man to take one more step back.

"Please, let's try and work something out." Jude took a step toward the man.

The man held his ground and pressed the

gun tighter against Lacey's head. Lacey closed her eyes, but this time she wasn't praying.

The laden branch above creaked as the snow started to slide. Jude lunged toward the man. The man stepped back, dragging Lacey with him. The snow fell on them, but because he was taller than Lacey, the bulk of it landed on the man's head. The man let go of Lacey. The moment of distraction was enough time for Jude to leap toward him and land a blow to his jaw and a second punch to his stomach.

The man held on to his gun. He aimed it at Jude and pulled the trigger. Lacey leaped on his back, which made the shot go wild. The man hit Lacey on the side of the head with the pistol. She toppled to the ground, not moving.

Shock spread through Jude at the sight of Lacey's still body. He lunged at the man before he had a chance to aim the gun at him. Both men fell on the snowy ground and rolled around.

The man was on top of Jude though he'd dropped his gun. He hit Jude several times in the face. Pain radiated through Jude's jaw. His vision blurred.

He slammed his fist into the man's stomach. And then sitting up, he put his hands on the man's shoulders and pushed him back. Jude tried to get to his feet. The man was already standing. Broad Shoulders glanced around searching for the gun. While Jude was still kneeling on the ground, the man kicked him in the stomach.

Lacey had begun to stir from the shock of the blow she'd sustained.

Once the man found his gun, they would both be dead.

He crawled toward Lacey.

The man stomped around kicking at the snow, still unable to find his gun.

Jude reached Lacey just as she opened her eyes. She sat up, taking in the scene. He scrambled to get to his feet and reached down to help her up.

The man's body slammed him, knocking him to the ground. Jude's face was buried in the snow. He heard punches being thrown. He flipped over. Despite a valiant effort, Lacey was no match for the man who had grabbed both her wrists as they faced each other.

Jude picked up a hefty branch and landed it across the man's back. The man remained upright but the blow was enough to stun him into inaction for a moment. Jude grabbed Lacey's hand and they raced back toward the SUV.

He could hear the man running behind them, right at their heels. Jude swung open the driver's side door. Lacey got in and scooted across the seat. As he moved to get into the car, the man grabbed him from behind. Jude swung around and punched him several times. The man wobbled and took a step back.

Jude got behind the wheel. Lacey had already started the SUV.

Broad Shoulders ran toward his own vehicle, stopping a moment to pick something up. He'd found his gun.

Lacey was safe with him. Now they just needed to get back to the road that led to Garnet. Their attacker ran toward his van. The shoulder they were parked on was too narrow to make a U-turn without sliding off the side or getting stuck in the deep snow. Jude sped ahead past the parked van, knowing that there had to be a place to turn around somewhere on the road.

Their attacker jumped into his car and raced after them.

Lacey gripped the dashboard and craned her neck. "How are we going to get turned around with him so close to us?"

Jude gripped the wheel and stared out at the flat terrain and the straight narrow road with a berm of snow on either side of it. He didn't know the answer to that question. His foot floored the accelerator and he sped down the road into the unknown.

Frantic, Lacey gulped in a breath of air and looked over her shoulder. The other car was drawing dangerously close to them. It was close enough that she could see the man behind the wheel, his teeth bared in rage.

The other car lurched forward and tapped their bumper. The impact jarred her body. She bit her tongue accidently. Her lower jaw stung with pain.

The man hit them a second time. Their car fishtailed, hitting one of the snowbanks. Jude held the wheel steady. "I can't shake him."

He sped up.

She feared they'd hit a patch of black ice. At this speed there was a danger of sliding into the snowbank. They came to a crossroads. Jude took a sharp left. The move put a little distance between them and the van.

They drove for several miles. The van remained behind them.

The tension in her chest made it hard to get a deep breath. "He's not going to give up until we're dead."

"I know," Jude said. "This road has to open up or lead somewhere."

"Jude, I saw something back at the gas station on television. Maria is home safe with her parents."

"That's good news. How did they get her back? Did George pay the ransom?"

"I don't know the details. All I saw was the tail end of the news story."

He glanced over at her. "Why do you look so grim?"

"Jude, I didn't know what George Ignatius looked like until I saw the news story. George was in Lodgepole. I saw him in the window of the house where Dale lived."

Jude shook his head. "Why would he lie to me? He called me from out of state."

"What if he had something to do with his own daughter's kidnapping?"

"That doesn't make any sense, Lacey. Why would he hire me if he was involved?"

Before she could answer. The attacker's car rammed their bumper once again. Jude swerved on the road, heading straight toward a snow pile. Her side of the car skimmed the edge of the snow berm. He straightened the wheel and righted the car.

The van remained close for another mile or so.

Jude slowed down. Up ahead, a farmer was moving his sheep across the road. The farmer along with a younger-looking man on a horse stood watch while a border collie ran circles around the sheep nipping at their heels. The men were some distance away from the road. Jude came to a full stop. The attacker stopped his car, as well. He wouldn't harm them with witnesses around.

"What if we asked that farmer for help?"

"We'd have to run all that way across the field out in the open." Jude rubbed his forehead and then tilted it toward the van. "We know he's already killed two other people. I don't see a farmhouse around here anywhere. It just seems like we'd be risking the guy's life and that kid's and I don't think we could get to them before the shooting started."

If they could get to town where there were lots of people, they'd be safe.

Jude checked the rearview mirror. "Looks like he's making a call. Must be cell service out here." He pointed at the phone on the floor of the passenger seat. "The sheriff's number was the last one I called. Tell him where we are and that we need help."

She took the phone. "I'm not sure where we are."

"I don't know exactly either. It was the first right turn off the main road after that gas station."

She laughed. "That's real precise."

In spite of their situation, he laughed too. "I know we've been driving for a long time. It might be hard to locate us. Maybe they can use GPS to find the cell." He glanced back at the van. "The sheriff needs to know. Just in case."

He didn't need to finish his sentence. She knew he meant just in case they didn't make it to Garnet. She spoke while the phone rang. "Wish I could remember the name of the gas station."

"There can't be that many between Lodgepole and Garnet."

Lacey spoke to the deputy who answered the phone, giving him all the information she had. She wasn't sure how to explain about seeing George Ignatius or if she even should. They had no evidence that George was connected to the kidnapping, only that he had lied about where he was at. The connection dropped out before she could explain. The last sheep made it across the road. Jude shifted into First and rolled forward. The van remained behind them the whole time though it seemed to be hanging back and just following them.

Lacey stared at the phone. "Do you suppose I can figure out where we are with the maps feature on this phone?"

Jude shrugged. "Worth a try."

The road widened a bit. A truck was in front of them for several miles and then turned off.

Lacey stared at the map on the phone. "It looks like there's a town not too far from here. It's called Stageline."

She looked up. Jude's face had drained of color. She stared at the road ahead where a car was parked facing forward, blocking the road. The road was so narrow, there was maybe a foot of clearance on either side.

"I guess we know who the guy in the van was talking to."

A chill ran down her spine as she stared straight ahead. Now she knew why the man hadn't tried to ram them once they were out of view of the farmer. "Looks like he called in reinforcements."

SEVENTEEN

Jude's heart pounded. The car up ahead completely blocked the road. There were two men in the front seat. The berm of snow on either side of the road was pretty steep. And there was still snow in the flat field beyond. The van behind them blocked the possibility of hitting Reverse and backing away.

"We don't have a lot of choice," Lacey said.

She must have been thinking the same thing he was thinking.

"Can you crawl in the backseat and get my gun?" Jude asked. "We might need it."

"Sure," she said.

Jude drew closer to the car speeding up. Maybe the guy would think he was playing chicken and back up. When he was within twenty feet of the other car, he turned the wheel sharply and gunned the engine, heading toward the open field.

The SUV hung at the top of the snow berm. One of the back wheels was spinning.

Lacey sat back up in the passenger seat, holding the holster in her lap. She glanced out her window. "One of the men is getting out of that car that is blocking the road."

Jude pressed the gas and turned the wheel. Three of thc tires still had traction. He could get them out of here. "You might want to pull that gun out of the holster." Jude spoke through gritted teeth.

He let up on the gas, hit Reverse, rolled back a foot and then sped forward. This time the SUV broke free. They lumbered over the berm and out into the field.

Lacey pulled the gun from the holster and ducked down. He caught only a glimpse of a man moving toward them before a bullet pinged off the metal of the car. He slipped down in the seat, as well.

The snow in the field was deep enough that it slowed them down, but he was still moving forward. In his rearview mirror, he could see the man with the gun climbing the berm and running after them.

The snow had grown heavy and slushy which slowed them even more.

The SUV chugged like they were driving with square tires. It took him a minute to realize it wasn't just the consistency of the snow that was slowing them down. One of their tires had deflated. The man with the gun must have shot at it. They weren't going to get much farther in the car.

"We're going to have to make a run for it." Jude turned the SUV so it was facing sideways. Lacey's side of the car was the farthest from the approaching gunman. They could use the car as cover until the shooter got beyond it. "Give me the gun."

She handed it to him and pushed open the car door, dropping to the ground. He crawled out behind her and caught up with her as she ran. The shooter was still about thirty feet from the car. Ahead of them lay an open field filled with melting snow.

The shooter had only a handgun which didn't have the same range as a rifle. As long as they kept twenty feet between them, he wouldn't be able to get a clean target. If he shot and ran at the same time, the possibility of getting an accurate shot was low. He'd have to stop and aim which meant they could put even more distance between them.

Along the road, the van was backing up, maybe to try and head them off if they tried to circle back to the road. Because there still wasn't a spot wide enough to turn around, the van had to continue to go backward.

The second car did not move.

They hurried as fast as they could. The bottom of his pant leg was weighed down from the moisture of the slushy snow. Jude glanced over his shoulder. The shooter had stopped and shoved his gun in his jacket. The van started to rumble forward, and the car shifted into Reverse.

A farm truck hauling a load of hay was behind the van. It was too far away for them to hope to wave it down. But the presence of the stranger was enough to make the men hide what they were up to.

The delay bought them precious minutes. They ran through the field. Jude veered off toward the east where a windbreak of trees stood in a straight line. The deciduous trees were barren and gray. Judging from the wide circumference of the trunks, the old oaks had to be at least fifty years old. They slipped in behind the trees. Both of them were gasping for air. Jude stared out at the field and then along the road. He couldn't see the van or the farmer's truck anymore, but the car was rolling down the road. It must have pulled off on a shoulder while driving backward and let the van and the farmer's truck go by.

The man with the gun was still headed across the field toward them.

Jude tugged on Lacey's sleeve. "Let's keep going." Though not a direct route, they were headed back in the direction they had come from toward the main road and the gas station though it had to be at least ten miles. They ran until the side road was no longer in view. The terrain turned from flat to rolling hills. Every time they came to the crest of a hill, Jude looked down to see the shooter still dogging them but never catching up. He was a lean man who appeared to be in very good shape. Was he just waiting for them to drop from exhaustion? Jude's leg muscles screamed from the amount of exertion.

They stopped only briefly to catch their breaths and then kept running. Their footsteps smacked through the damp heavy snow. He was grateful for his waterproof boots or his feet would have been as soaked as his pant legs.

He wondered if they would just be running forever, never being caught, but never able to get away either. Up ahead, he saw a field populated with huge round hay bales. This might be the chance they were looking for. They could hide behind one of the bales and try to ambush the shooter. Or, maybe the shooter would run right by them.

After glancing over his shoulder and not seeing their pursuer, he sprinted toward the middle of the field. Lacey ran beside him. Their boots made squishy sounds on the half-melted snow. He crouched behind a bale and Lacey slipped in beside him, pressed close to his back. He pulled the gun from his waist-band. He could feel Lacey's breath on his neck and the heat of her touch as she rested her hand on his upper shoulder.

Time seemed to slow down as he watched and listened. The rhythm of Lacey's breathing matched his own. His leg muscles started to cramp. He switched to a more comfortable position on his knees which meant his pants would get even more wet.

Lacey whispered in his ear. "I'll keep a lookout on the other side of the bale. I'll signal you if I see him coming."

Jude nodded. The less they talked, the better. The guy might have figured out their plan and was already creeping through the field.

Jude angled his head around the bale so he could see more. His gaze moved from one open area to another and then he studied each of the hay bales. A crow fluttered down on top of one of the other bales picking at whatever morsels of food he could find.

The distant cawing of other crows filled the air. Jude glanced at the slow-moving clouds in the blue sky. The calm he saw there stood in sharp contrast to his pounding heart and tensed muscles.

He turned to glance back at Lacey. His heart froze. She wasn't there. He had a moment of fear that she'd been snatched. But no one could be that quiet. She would have put up a fight. She'd moved for some reason.

He studied the area around him. Lacey stuck her head out from the side of a bale not too far from him and gave him the okay sign. She had probably reasoned that they could see more if they were split up behind different bales.

The wind ruffled his hair and he adjusted his grip on the gun. The crow on top of the bale flapped away. Jude went on high alert as his gaze darted everywhere. The crow may just have had his fill of grain or he may have been frightened by something.

Jude heard movement, footsteps, off to his side. He rose up and lifted his gun. Lacey had run from one bale to the next. His breath hitched. Now he knew what she was doing. She must have spotted the shooter and was making herself bait to draw him out. No wonder she hadn't said anything. Making her a target was a plan he never would have agreed to.

Jude sprinted toward another bale. He heard swishing movements but couldn't see anything.

At the sound of the first gunshot, his heart squeezed tight and he prayed for Lacey's safety.

Jude sprinted toward the next bale, still not seeing anything.

Lacey was pretty sure that first shot had lodged in the hay bale she was hiding behind. So the shooter had seen her. Her heartbeat drummed in her ears as she rose up and prepared to run to the next bale. She could not see the shooter or Jude, but she heard squishy footsteps all around her.

Crouching low, she sprinted out into the open. The next bale was only fifteen feet away, but it felt like a thousand miles while she was vulnerable and exposed. She was sure that Jude would realize what her plan was. As she ran, she looked from side to side. She caught a flash of movement. Someone slipping behind a bale not too far from her. He'd disappeared before she could tell if it was Jude or the shooter.

She ran to hide behind the next bale but

stuttered in her step. The shooter with his back to her crouched one bale away. She scrambled to the side of her bale so he wouldn't see her. That meant that it was Jude who had gone behind the other bale. Their positioning formed a sort of triangle. Jude at the apex of the triangle and the shooter and her at the lower angles.

Lacey took in a breath and rested her palm against her raging heart. She could try to jump the shooter from the back. But if he heard her coming, he could turn and shoot her. At that close a range the shot was bound to be fatal.

She crept around to the other side of the bale that was closer to where she'd seen Jude. She sprinted out toward the next bale, pressing against the side of it that was the farthest away from the one where she'd seen the shooter.

Fear raged through her at the same time she felt a surge of strength. She ran to the next bale. She was one bale away from where she'd seen Jude when a volley of gunfire shattered the silence around her.

She pressed into the bale as terror froze her in place. The straw was itchy against the back of her neck. A deafening silence fell around her. The beating of her own heart seemed to

be the only thing she could hear. And then she
detected the distant cawing of the crows and
felt the breeze on her face. She shook herself
free of the paralysis, scrambled toward the
edge of the bale and peered out to see if she
could figure out what had happened.

She looked everywhere, not seeing or hearing anything. She feared that Jude lay on the
cold wet ground bleeding to death, and the
shooter was just waiting for her to find him
so he could take her out too.

She thought she heard footsteps off to the
side of her. She ran the other way toward the
nearest bale. Her own footsteps seemed to
be getting louder. She slowed and stepped
more lightly.

She pressed against the side of the cylindri-
cal hay bale and tilted her head to the sky and
listened. She'd worked her way almost to the
end of the field. Ahead she could see another
windbreak of trees and a barbed wire fence.
She wasn't leaving without Jude. She had to
know what had happened. If the shooter had
taken him out, he was probably still stalking
the field looking for her.

She crawled to the top of the hay bale,
lifting her head only slightly to try to get a
view of the field. One more shot was fired,
followed by the deafening quiet, no cries of

pain, no indication that anyone had been hit. She recoiled but managed a deep breath, still studying the field. She could guess the direction the shot had come from, several bales back from where she'd just been.

To run to where the shot had been fired from meant she might be running directly toward the shooter. She waited and watched. In the midst of this standoff, someone had to move sooner or later. Even slight movement caused the straw to make noise. She pressed her belly against it and willed herself to be still.

Her gaze darted from one bale to the next and then to the open areas. After what felt like forever, she saw Jude's head for only a moment before he was hidden again.

Heart racing, she crawled down and ran to the edge of field on the side where she'd spotted Jude. She risked running into the shooter, but she worried that Jude would be distracted wondering about her safety. If they were together, they could take on the shooter.

Jude was three hay bales up from the edge of the field. She darted to the end of the first cylinder of straw, stopping only to take in a deep breath before she ran to the next one. Her fingers pulled straw out to release some of the tension building up inside of her. Her stomach had coiled into a tight knot.

She prayed that Jude hadn't already repositioned again. This deadly game could go on forever if he had. She ran toward the last place she'd seen Jude.

When she got there…the space was empty.

She heard footsteps behind her. Before she could turn around, an object hit her head and a view of the ground filled her vision.

EIGHTEEN

"Jude, I have your girlfriend. Come and get her."

The mocking tone of the shooter tore Jude to pieces. Gritting his teeth, he squeezed his eyes shut.

"I'll give you to a count of ten and then I'm going to put a bullet in her."

Was it possible the shooter was lying to lure him out? Jude stood up and shouted, "I need to hear her voice."

"That's not possible. I call the terms of this arrangement."

Was Lacey already dead? Or maybe unconscious.

Judging from the volume of the shooter's voice. Jude was within one or two bales of where the man was. He took in a deep breath to try to loosen the tightness he felt in his chest. He peered around the bale where he was hiding, still not seeing anything. He didn't have a clear plan, all he knew was that he needed to get to Lacey.

If she was conscious, close and not being held at gunpoint, she would have heard the shouting and responded in some way to warn him. He studied the field and the fence and trees beyond. Could she be hiding out there?

Too many questions, too many unknowns. He hurried to the next bale in the general direction the man's voice had come from. He ran to another bale and looked out. Adrenaline surged through him as he raised his gun. The shooter was turned sideways. Lacey lay on the ground beside him.

Before he could pull the trigger, the shooter raised his gun. Jude dove behind the bale for cover and fired a shot. When he looked out, the man was no longer out in the open. Lacey lay motionless on the cold wet snow. No doubt, the shooter was somewhere he could watch her, so running to rescue her would only get them both killed.

A strange mumbling reached his ears. Jude lifted his chin, listening. It sounded like the shooter was on a phone. The voice grew louder then softer. Like he was pacing.

He touched his own pocket where his phone should have been. It must still be on the console of the SUV from when he'd had Lacey call in to the sheriff.

From the sound of the voice, the man was getting farther away. That didn't make sense. Wouldn't the shooter at least be where he could see Lacey?

Lacey's body jerked. She must be coming around. The intense need to run to her, to make sure she was safe, overwhelmed him. The shooter had to be using her as bait. Jude glanced all around, not seeing any movement or any sign of the other man. The voice had faded altogether.

Lacey stirred even more. Her legs moved and she lifted her head slightly. She must be cold lying there on the ground for so long. She opened her eyes. Her expression changed when she saw him. Her features softened, and warmth seemed to come into her eyes.

He rose up to run to her when he heard footsteps behind him. He turned but saw no one. The man was on the other side of the hay bale. Jude glanced over at Lacey, who was still struggling to get to her feet. Her hand went to the side of her head.

The next few minutes seemed to unfold in slow motion. The broad-shouldered man came out of nowhere and grabbed Lacey before she could get to her feet. He pulled her by her hair and held a gun to her stomach. A look of terror crossed her features as she reached out a hand toward Jude and was dragged away. He jerked to move toward her.

Jude had been so focused on Lacey and what the shooter was up to, he hadn't seen the van driven by Broad Shoulders lumbering across the field to park behind the windbreak.

Broad Shoulders lifted his chin in a challenging way as his gaze darted toward the gun that was held on Lacey. Jude watched in horror as the man's finger moved to the trigger. Lacey's eyes grew wide with fear.

Breath caught in Jude's throat.

Broad Shoulders looked out beyond Jude. His grimace went slack as he withdrew the gun from view but still was controlling her by pushing the gun into her back. Jude glanced over his shoulder.

The farmer they'd seen earlier had driven into the adjoining field where cattle rested. His truck rolled forward while he threw rectangular straw bales off the back of it.

Jude felt something hard push against his back. A gun. The shooter who had chased them across the field spoke in a low voice. "Get moving and don't try anything."

"You won't shoot me," Jude said and tilted

his head toward where the farmer was. "I know you don't want witnesses."

"Shut up," the man who had chased them said. "It would be nothing for me to drag you behind that hay bale and put a bullet through you."

That might be true. But the farmer would still remember seeing two strange men in the field and if a body was found later, he would connect the dots. Broad Shoulders had disappeared behind the windbreak. The van was nearly camouflaged by the bare trees. He didn't see the other car or its driver anywhere. Maybe he had left.

"Okay, I'll go." All Jude knew was that Lacey had just been loaded into that van. He wasn't about to abandon her. Even if he could get away and get the farmer's attention, Lacey would still be held captive. She would be killed and her body dumped somewhere else.

The farmer, focused on feeding the cows, had not looked in their direction other than a quick glance. Men and a woman in a field had to look out of place.

They walked across the snowy muddy field to where the van was. The shooter swung open the side door of the van and shoved Jude inside. Lacey was there. Her back pressed against the wall of the van. Her hands tied in front of her.

"Stay away from her. No talking."

The man who had captured Jude got into the passenger seat of the van and slammed the door.

"Thought I was going to have to leave without you," Broad Shoulders said.

"Like you would," the second man, who had buggy eyes, said. His red hair stuck out beneath his winter hat.

There were no windows in the back of the van and Jude couldn't see much out the front window without lifting up. He raised his eyebrows as a way of communicating with Lacey. She gave a slight nod in response.

"What are we supposed to do with them now?"

"I'm sure boss wants us to find a place to get rid of them."

Jude wondered who the *boss* was referring to. Had it been the man who was the driver in the other car? Jude had not seen him at all. Was it like Lacey had speculated, George Ignatius had conspired in the kidnapping of his own daughter?

"Off the road somewhere should be fine. Just find a concealed area," Bug Eyes said.

The words sent a chill through Jude. Did they have only minutes to live?

"Don't you think you should tie him up too?"

"Why? This will be over soon enough. Let's just get this done. Then, I want to go into town and grab a burger."

The callousness of the men sent a new shock wave of fear through him. His hands weren't tied. He had to act. He glanced around in search of a weapon. Lacey seemed to understand, as well. She looked from side to side and shook her head.

The van went from rolling smoothly to bumping along. He didn't have much time. He jumped up and reached for the driver, knowing the other man had a gun. All the same, if they were distracted by a potential wreck, he and Lacey might have a fighting chance.

Lacey jumped up as well, moving toward the man in the passenger seat. Jude wrapped his hands around the neck of the driver while Lacey pummeled the passenger with her bound hands.

The driver took his hands off the wheel in an attempt to free himself from Jude's stranglehold. The van swerved.

Broad Shoulders wrestled free of Jude's hold. The passenger had subdued Lacey by gripping her bound hands and pushing her down. Through the windshield, Jude saw the farmer in the truck driving toward them.

With Lacey under control, both men pounced on Jude.

The passenger, the man with buggy eyes, glanced nervously through the windshield. "Get him out of sight," Broad Shoulders said.

Jude felt a hard object hit the side of his head. Black dots filled the edges of his vision as his view of the orange carpet in the back of the van loomed toward him.

He heard Lacey scream.

"Shut her up before that farmer gets here."

With his cheek pressed against the carpet, he saw feet moving toward where Lacey lay. His eyelids were as heavy as lead. He fought to remain alert. The darkness closed in on him.

Lacey tried to crawl away as Bug Eyes lunged toward her. He placed his hand over her mouth and slid out of view behind the seat. Up front, the driver rolled down the window. "Hey there."

There was a pause and then an unfamiliar voice spoke up. "Is everything okay here?" That must be the farmer she'd seen driving toward them. His voice was filled with suspicion.

"Oh, sure. I'm just a little lost. I'm not from around here…trying to get to town."

"Weren't you with some other people?"

"They're laying down in the back. We've been driving for hours. That's why we were out in that field. I'm sure you saw us there. We just needed to stretch our legs is all. We didn't mean to trespass."

Lacey twisted from side to side, trying to escape. She reached her free hand up to claw at the man's fingers. If she could just get his hand off her mouth, she'd be able to cry out. The man pressed even harder against her mouth.

Again, there was hesitation before the farmer said anything. "You sure everything is all right?"

"Oh sure, if you could just point me toward the nearest town."

"Stageline is just up the road a piece."

"Thanks."

Lacey heard the window close. The driver shifted into Reverse. Bug Eyes released his hold on her and jerked her around. He removed a winter scarf from around his neck and used it as a gag.

He put his face very close to hers. "Just in case you get any ideas."

Before taking his place in the front seat, he tied up Jude, as well.

After a few minutes, the driver spoke up as he glanced in his rearview mirror. "Would you look at that. That stupid farmer is following us."

"What kind of do-gooder citizen is he?" Bug Eyes said.

"Well, I guess we got to go into Stageline or he's going to report us. I was hungry anyway," Broad Shoulders said. "What are we supposed to do with those two?"

"We could shoot them now and dispose of the bodies later."

Lacey's heart beat faster at the suggestion. Sweat trickled down her back. She pressed her head against the back of the driver's seat.

"I can't risk being caught in a car with two bodies. Mr. Do-gooder Farmer already thinks we're up to something. He can identify this vehicle. He's probably written down the license number. He knows what I look like. I'm not going back to prison. That was not the deal I made."

"We need to have a plan here," Bug Eyes said. "First thing, we shake Farmer Joe. Do you think he'll give up once he sees we're turning into town?"

"I don't like being in the van with these

two. This is way more than I bargained for. I was supposed to be out of the country by now. This whole thing is a mess. Get on the phone to the boss," Broad Shoulders said.

Lacey listened while Bug Eyes told the man on the other end of the line what was going on. "Look, we're being followed. This is way more than we signed up for. Way more than we agreed to. Okay fine, soon as we throw this guy off, they're your problem. You need to get over here to this town... Stageline." He turned the phone off.

The van picked up speed as it turned onto what must have been a paved road.

"Do you suppose that farmer has already phoned in to the law?" The driver sounded nervous.

"Could be," the passenger said.

A tiny bit of hope blossomed for Lacey. The sheriff in Garnet knew what was going on. She didn't know if Stageline was big enough to have any law enforcement. If a call came in, maybe the sheriff in Garnet would put two and two together and know where to look for them.

"All he has to go on at this point is his own suspicions. He's probably following us to see if he can find a reason to report us."

"I say we can't take any chances," Bug Eyes said.

The men drove on in silence. Several times Bug Eyes turned in the passenger seat to check on her and Jude, who had not stirred from being unconscious yet. He raised his gun in her direction to let her know she dared not try anything.

The van slowed down. They must have been within the town limits.

"Put that gun away," the driver said. "I don't want anyone seeing you with it through the window."

"So what do we do now?"

"We told that farmer we were going to find a bite to eat, so let's do that." The turn signal beat out a droning rhythm. When she lifted her head, she could see some houses and a gas station.

The passenger twisted in his seat. The gun was in his lap. His face was red with rage. "Get back down."

The two men were clearly on edge.

"I suppose it's too much to hope for a drive-through in a town this size," Broad Shoulders said.

"Over there." The passenger pointed through the window. "You can get us some food to go. I'll wait here and watch these two."

"Is that farmer still following us?"

"He's parked. Watching us from across the street."

"Suppose he's not going to give up until he sees at least one of us go inside," the driver said. "Watch her close. I don't want any chance that she can draw someone's attention."

Bug Eyes crawled back and put his face very close to hers. "Don't try anything."

"I'll order something quick. I want to ditch these guys," Broad Shoulders said. "This is the end of the line for me. I need to get out of the country before this whole thing blows up. Once I got that kid off the mountain that was supposed to be the end of my job."

Broad Shoulders left the car. She wiggled snakelike across the carpet. She could just lift her head above the console between the seats.

"Hey, get down," the man in the passenger seat said.

There was only one other vehicle in the parking lot and it was parked at the other end. She slipped out of view. It seemed there was no way to get anyone's attention and no way to escape the vehicle.

With her bound hands, she reached out and touched Jude's head, brushing the lock of golden-brown hair out of his eyes. Though she could see his pulse throbbing on the side of his neck, it concerned her that he had been out for so long.

She scooted a little closer to him, knowing they both did not have long to live.

NINETEEN

Jude awoke to the sound of Bug Eyes and Broad Shoulders talking. The tension in the van was palpable. Lacey sat with her hands tied. She smiled at him when he opened his eyes.

"I think that highway patrol car is following us," Broad Shoulders said. "There is no way we can pull off and get rid of these guys."

"There hasn't been any place for him to turn off. It's miles of straight road. Maybe he's just headed in the same direction as us."

Broad Shoulders sped up. "Wrong. His lights are flashing."

Bug Eyes glanced in the side-view mirror. "We can't be caught with these guys. This was supposed to be an easy job."

"I don't like this. I'm not going back to prison." Broad Shoulders accelerated even more and then took a tight turn. "This is way more than I signed up for. We're not that far from where the boss is. I say we shake this guy and make those two in the back his problem."

"Okay, if that is what you want to do," Bug Eyes said. He noticed that Jude was awake. He aimed the gun at him. "I'm watching you."

Jude caught a glimpse of a sign that said they were in Stageline. Broad Shoulders took several sharp turns, weaving through city and residential streets. He drove for another ten minutes.

Broad Shoulders checked his rearview mirror. His shoulders relaxed. "Good, looks like we lost our friendly law enforcement."

The van climbed a long winding hill and came to a stop. Jude lifted his chin. He could just see a garage door and a large cabin. A car that looked a lot like the one that had dropped Bug Eyes off was parked outside.

Bug Eyes opened his door and disappeared, then returned a moment later. Broad Shoulders rolled down the window.

"He's not happy about seeing us. But he says bring them in. Hide the van in the garage just in case that cop gets eager again and starts to search this neighborhood."

Lacey and Jude were pulled out of the van. "Put them in different rooms so they don't get any ideas," Broad Shoulders said. Lacey's eyes filled with fear as they were both brought into the kitchen and then she was taken to another room. He was shoved in the room next to the kitchen. The man they referred to as the boss had yet to make an appearance.

The curtains were drawn in the room where he'd been tossed, and the lights were out. His hands were tied in front of him. Though his head hurt from the blow he'd received, he pushed himself into a sitting position. He wondered where they'd taken Lacey.

He waited for his eyes to adjust to the darkness. He was in the rec room of some sort of cabin. The heads of animals were mounted on the walls. He had been placed on a couch. There was a shelf with games and books and a big fireplace that took up most of the wall. There were no personal items anywhere and the decor, from the leather couch to the cow skin rug and the stuffed animal heads, suggested a Western theme. He speculated that he might be in a vacation rental.

He could hear an argument taking place in the next room. Broad Shoulders yelling about how he had already done the job he was paid to do. Jude heard stomping and a door slamming. A vehicle started up and peeled away.

He rose to his feet. His legs were stiff and numb. He pulled aside a curtain and stared out into darkness. Off in the distance, he saw the twinkling lights of several other houses. A car whizzed by, headed down the hill. That must be Broad Shoulders leaving. Even farther away was a cluster of lights that suggested a small town. Again, he wondered what had happened to Lacey. He tried to open the window thinking he might crawl out. He pulled the latch forward but with his hands bound was unable to lift the window.

Voices in the next room drew his attention. He stumbled across the wood floor. When he tried the doorknob, it was locked. He pressed his ear close to the door. This time whoever was talking must be right outside the door. He could hear them more clearly.

"We can't do away with them here. It doesn't matter that I didn't rent this place under my name. My DNA is all over this place. There can be no link between me and their deaths because all of that will point the finger at me being involved with Maria's kidnapping."

Jude slid down to the floor. He knew that voice. George Ignatius. His words confirmed what Lacey had speculated about.

"Okay, so we move them and dispose of them," said a second voice that belonged to Bug Eyes.

"They've seen too much. If law enforcement is out looking for them, we have to hurry," George said. "Reed took my car. You're going to have to take the van. Get rid of the bodies and get rid of the van. I'll make arrangements for you to be picked up."

Reed must be Broad Shoulders.

There was a moment's hesitation before Bug Eyes responded. "So all the risk is still on me. No way."

"I'll make it worth your while."

"There is not enough money in the world at this point."

"Fine, I'll help you," said George.

"And double my fee," said Bug Eyes.

"I don't have much choice at this point," said George.

One of them stomped across the floorboards coming closer. Jude darted back to the couch. The door swung open. George Ignatius stepped into the room and stalked over to where Jude sat.

Muscular and over six feet tall, George was an imposing figure with his jet-black hair and angular features. "You must have heard the conversation."

"I get it." Jude cleared his throat. "I'm going to die."

George lifted his chin in a show of dominance. "Do you think I'd be standing here in front of you if that wasn't the case?"

But it seemed as though George's goons were losing their enthusiasm.

"Why did you hire me?"

"I had to make it look like I was trying to get Maria back even if the kidnappers threatened to kill her if I got the FBI involved." George crossed his arms. "I have to say I'm impressed with you. I didn't think a washed-up cop would get as far as you did."

The remark was meant to hurt, but it didn't. He knew he was no longer the guy who had given up on life. Being with Lacey had renewed his faith and his confidence. And all that they had been through and overcome showed him he wasn't washed-up. "Why kidnap your own daughter?"

"She was never harmed, and she was never afraid." George's words sounded defensive as he took a step toward him. "My wife holds the purse strings. Let's just say there were some big expenses she couldn't know about."

Jude could feel the rage toward George growing inside him even as he fought off the rising fear. What kind of evil man would put his own daughter through such a trial just to get money from his wife?

George narrowed his eyes at Jude as he

leaned toward him. Even in the dim light, Jude could see the wildness in his eyes. Greed was a funny thing that consumed the hearts of men. "I hadn't counted on that snowstorm stranding me and delaying the ransom drop-off and Maria's return."

"Where are your wife and daughter now?"

"They're waiting for me back home. I needed to make sure all the loose ends on this thing were wrapped up. They think I'm on a business trip," George said. "Soon as I get rid of you and that woman, we'll be one big happy family again."

Jude swallowed, trying to produce some moisture in his mouth. The rising panic would not own him, not today or any day. Adrenaline pumped through his body. He jumped up and, using his head as a blunt object, slammed into George's chest.

It was wrong, immoral to do what George had done. A desire for justice gave Jude strength.

The move knocked George off his feet. He fell backward on his behind. Rage over what George had done surged through him. Jude jumped on the older man and pummeled him in the face and stomach with his bound hands.

He knew too that the rage was toward himself for having fallen for George's deception.

Bug Eyes ran into the room and pulled Jude off George.

George rose to his feet, squared his shoulders and brushed his sleeves off. "Get him and the girl loaded up. We'll get to where there are no witnesses and the bodies won't be found or connected to this place and then we need to make sure that van is sunk in a lake or set on fire."

Jude twisted back and forth fighting to break free of the hold that Bug Eyes had on him.

George glared at Bug Eyes. "This wasn't supposed to go down this way. You shouldn't have come here."

"We did the best we could," Bug Eyes said through gritted teeth. "We didn't know they'd put up such a fight."

Jude sensed the tension between the two men.

"We'll take the back roads where the van isn't likely to be spotted," George said. "Let's go. We need to discuss the best way to get rid of them and get some things together. I don't want to be linked to this." He stomped out of the room.

Bug Eyes shoved Jude back in the room. Jude heard the lock on the door click shut as he slumped down on the couch. He was grateful that Lacey was still alive. Where they were keeping her, he didn't know. Probably somewhere in the house in another locked room.

His head was still throbbing. He had to find some way to get Lacey and him out of here. There were houses just down the road. He rose to his feet, heading over to the bookcase that contained games and books. He walked the room looking for some way to cut through the rope that confined his hands.

The rock on the stone fireplace would maybe provide a sharp enough edge to free him. He positioned himself so he could rub the rope back and forth on the corner rock. How much time did he have? Ten minutes? Half an hour?

He had no way of knowing.

He rubbed the rope with a furious intensity. He could hear George and Bug Eyes arguing in the next room. The second man was demanding more money.

Dale and Mr. Wilson were killed by the man they called Reed. He hoped that man would not get away. Jude doubted the man who was still with George would turn him in no matter how mad he was about the situation. Only he and Lacey could tell the story that would put George and his associates behind bars.

He prayed that that secret would not die with him and Lacey. They had to get out of here and tell the sheriff all they knew and all they had seen. Justice would not be served until George Ignatius was behind bars.

Lacey stared at the ceiling in the bedroom where she'd been locked. She could hear two men downstairs arguing. Her hands were tied in front of her. At least they had taken the gag out of her mouth. She'd been placed in a chair. The curtains were drawn, but she could see through a slit that it was nighttime.

She'd watched them haul Jude away, but she had no idea where he was in the cabin.

She steeled herself and rose to her feet. She walked toward the dresser and pulled open a drawer, which contained a Bible and a brochure about the area. Apparently, they were in one of the guest cabins outside of Stageline. The guest cabins connected with a golf course and indoor swimming facility. She walked into the bathroom. Opening drawers with her hands tied was a bit of a challenge. She found nothing that would help her cut her hands free. The personal items in the shower indicated the bathroom had been used recently. In desperation, she kicked over the garbage can hoping to find a used razor.

Nothing but paper. She looked around. The metal frame that surrounded the glass shower door was bent up in one spot. She placed her hands on it and sawed back and forth cutting through the rope.

The sound of footsteps coming up the stairs sent a surge of terror through her. She heard the door unlocking just as she locked the bathroom door. She opened the bathroom window.

"Hey. What do you think you're doing?" Bug Eyes pounded on the bathroom door and jiggled the doorknob.

She flipped open the window and pushed the screen out.

A tremendous thud shook the whole room. The man seemed to be slamming his body against the door. She stared down at the dark ground below. Two stories was a ways to jump, but what choice did she have?

She climbed out of the window and hung on for a moment before letting go, praying for a soft landing. Some barren bushes broke her fall but scratched her up. The man must have given up breaking the door down and was headed down the stairs and outside. She rolled toward the darkness of the bushes that surrounded the house.

She heard two men shouting at each other.

One of them came and stood beneath the porch light. It was the man she'd seen in Lodgepole and then later on the television, George Ignatius.

Another man, the bug-eyed one who had been in the van, came up to George again. They shouted at each other before resuming their search for her.

She glanced around. The lights of other houses glowed, the nearest one was maybe a quarter mile away as the crow flies.

They could get to help, but first she had to find Jude. She ran toward the house, peering inside. She saw a kitchen and living room. Then she came to a room where the curtains were drawn but the window was open. She stuck her head in. It was some sort of rec room with a fireplace, couch and shelf filled with books and games. No one was inside.

Footsteps pounded off to the side. She glanced around spotting a tarp, which she rolled under just as the footsteps reached the side of the house she was on.

"She has to be here somewhere," George said. "Find her."

"How do you know she's not already headed down the hill to get help?"

"She wouldn't leave without him."

More footsteps. "I think we got a problem. Looks like he's gotten out too."

"Find them. Find them both." George's voice filled with rage. "I'll see if I can spot them headed down the road or anywhere around it." George lifted a gun and then shoved it in his waistband.

Lacey lifted the tarp to a view of a pair of white cowboy boots that belonged to Bug Eyes. The man paced.

The man stopped with the boots facing her. Then took a step toward the tarp. Her breath caught in her throat. Of course, the tarp looked like a good hiding place. There was no way to escape.

The boots stopped about three feet from the tarp, turned slightly and then Bug Eyes ran off. Something had caught his attention.

Heart racing, she lifted the tarp. The cold night chilled her. She still had on her winter coat but no hat or gloves. Lacey hurried toward the edge of the property where there was a fence. She circled around one side of the house searching for Jude. She stayed back in the shadows knowing that she might encounter Bug Eyes.

She came around to the second side of the house. Jude might be hiding in the shadows, as well. How were they ever going to find each other? Maybe the smart thing to do would be to head down the road but not where George would see her. She could get help. But would she get back in time to save Jude? It was too risky. She had to find Jude.

Still not seeing anything, she ran around to the next side of the house. From this vantage point on the edge of the property, she could see George walking down the road shining his flashlight. He aimed the flashlight in the bushes. Her breath hitched. Had he seen movement? Was Jude down there?

She'd circled around to three sides of the property and still had not run into Bug Eyes. Maybe he'd gone back inside for some reason.

Lacey ran around to the fourth side of the house. No Jude and no Bug Eyes. She was facing the back door. She saw movement inside. A man crouching as he walked past the kitchen window in the dimly lit house. She could not tell if it was Jude or the other man. Both men must be inside.

She stepped into a mudroom area. She heard footsteps in the adjoining room which had to be the kitchen.

Lacey pressed against the wall, trying to find the courage to step into the dark kitchen and face the danger there.

TWENTY

Jude slipped out of the kitchen into the living room. All the lights were off, but the curtains were not drawn like they had been in the rec room. He hurried to hide behind a couch just as he heard footsteps behind him entering the living room.

"I know you're in here," Bug Eyes said.

Jude pressed against the side of the couch knowing that any noise would give him away. Bug Eyes must have seen Jude through the window when he was upstairs looking for Lacey. Jude had gotten out of the house through the window, but he'd slipped back in to search for Lacey through an unlocked door on the main floor. When he'd looked upstairs for Lacey, he found a room with a broken bathroom door, an open window and the cut rope that had bound Lacey's hands. Speculating that she must have gotten out too, he hurried downstairs to find her but had encountered Bug Eyes before he could get outside.

The man switched on the lights.

Jude braced himself. It was only a matter of seconds before he was found. He listened to the slow footsteps. From where he crouched, he watched the man as he checked behind the curtains. The man still had his gun in his waistband. His white cowboy boots pounded on the wood floor like a funeral dirge.

Jude crawled to the front of the couch, staying low. He had a straight shot to the door that led into the kitchen. Could he get there before the man pulled his gun and aimed? He doubted that Bug Eyes cared about George not wanting the bodies connected to this rental. It was the only option he had. He took in a breath and prepared to run when the lights in the kitchen flashed on and off.

Bug Eyes cursed and ran into the kitchen just as the lights were turned out again. Jude heard a muffled thud and then the man yelled. Leaping to his feet, Jude ran into the kitchen. Lacey hit the man with a golf club. The man grabbed the golf club and yanked it out of Lacey's hand. Jude dove toward the man before he could attack Lacey, balling his hand into a fist and smashing it against the man's jaw. In response, Bug Eyes swung the golf club and hit Jude in the shoulder. Pain vibrated down Jude's arm making his fingers tingle.

Lacey jumped into the fray slapping Bug Eyes on the face and chest. The blows were not strong enough to disable the man, but they served as a distraction. Jude maneuvered around him and reached for his gun. Before he could get it, the man had swung around unleashing the full force of his rage on Jude. Hitting him on the head and in the stomach before pulling his gun and aiming it at Jude.

The man spoke to Lacey but kept his eyes on Jude. "Take one step closer to me, and he gets a bullet through his chest."

Lacey put her hands up.

"George doesn't want us to die in this house," Jude said. "Those are his orders."

Bug Eyes took a moment to respond. "I'm tired of his orders." He tilted his head and pointed the gun at Lacey. "Go and stand by him."

The only chink in the armor of George's plan was that his goons were losing heart. One man had driven off and the other's enthusiasm for helping George was fading.

Keeping her arms in the air, she walked across the floor and positioned herself by Jude.

The man was breathless from the altercation and his face was red. He pulled the phone out of his front shirt pocket, still keeping the gun on them.

"Phone George and tell him to get back here." He extended the phone in Lacey's direction. "It's the last number I called, listed just as GI."

Lacey took the phone and pressed the required buttons. She cleared her throat. "He has us both. You can come back and stop looking."

Jude could hear George's laughter even though he wasn't on speaker. Once George got back and loaded them in the van, it would be all over for them. Their bodies might not be found for months or maybe never.

Lacey hung up the phone.

"Good girl." Bug Eyes never took his eyes off Jude, probably judging him to be the bigger threat. "Now put the phone back in my pocket and don't try anything."

Lacey did what the man asked. And then stepped back toward Jude. The man indicated the kitchen chairs. "Why don't you both sit down, turn the chairs so they face me?"

With the gun pointed at them, they had no choice but to do what he requested.

They had only minutes before George got back and it would all be over.

"George has put you through a lot," Jude

said. He knew he couldn't win the man over, but maybe he could weaken his resolve.

"He's paying me extra."

"Yes, but is it worth it?" Lacey said. She must have picked up on his game plan. He doubted the man would turn on George, but maybe they could make him let his guard down enough for them to overpower him. "Your partner left, didn't he?"

"Yeah, he got mad and took off," Bug Eyes said.

"What is your name, anyway?" Jude said.

"Does it matter?" The man lowered the gun a little.

Jude could tell from the man's body language that he was softening toward them. All the same, they didn't have much time.

"You look tired," Lacey said. "George is asking a lot of you."

The remark made the man's posture soften even more.

While the man focused on Lacey, Jude glanced around the room to where the golf club lay. He couldn't get to it before Bug Eyes pulled the trigger.

Jude waited for the moment when the man's gaze rested fully on Lacey. Jude grabbed a chair and swung at the man. Lacey dove for the golf club. The man let go of the gun as he fell to his knees and it slid across the floor out of sight. They heard a door open.

George would be coming through the mud-room and into the kitchen any second. They'd have to take the other door. The man remained on his knees, conscious but dazed. As they hurried toward the other door, which was actually the front door, Jude heard George step into the kitchen.

The door they went through looked out on the golf course and several outbuildings which were only silhouettes in the nighttime darkness.

They ran across the snowy rolling field toward the first building. When he peered inside, he saw that it was a storage area for golf carts. The door was locked.

They had to find a way to get turned around so they could run to one of the houses and get help. Maybe there were other houses connected to other holes on the golf course, but he could not see any lights that indicated that.

When he looked out the side of the building closest to the rental house, he saw one man moving toward them on foot. That meant the other man, probably George, must be watching for them to try to connect with the road that led to the other houses.

"The brochure I saw said that these are

vacation rentals that had a golf course and swimming facilities." Lacey pointed. "That other building must be where the swimming pool is."

"We don't have much choice." Jude grabbed Lacey's hand and squeezed it before taking off running.

The half-melted snow had crusted up and frozen in the low night temperatures. They slid but did not fall down. When Jude glanced over his shoulder, he could see a man drawing closer to them. Bug Eyes ran at a steady pace toward them, shining a flashlight.

Jude hurried around to the far side of the building hoping to see light that might indicate a house on this side of the building. He saw only a line of trees and more rolling hills where the golf course was spread out.

Lacey shook the doorknob. "Maybe we can hide if we can find a way in." The door didn't budge. "This is a big building. There are two of us and only one of him. Maybe we can take him out before George gets here."

Jude cupped a hand on Lacey's shoulder. "He's getting closer."

She stopped shaking the door and followed him to the side of the building. He crouched along the wall of the brick building. There was a concrete pad connected to part of the facility. They could hear footsteps as Bug Eyes drew near.

"Let's split up. You go that way around. Maybe we can catch him." If they could get one guy out of commission, it would be that much easier to get to help.

Lacey disappeared into the darkness. Jude turned back around and headed in the direction that he'd heard the footsteps. He pressed his back against the brick building and eased around the corner. Bug Eyes was standing there looking out with his back to Jude. Jude took cautious footsteps, trying to hide beneath the shadows that the eaves on the building provided. The man stepped away from the building but continued to look in the opposite direction from where Jude was. He thought he heard another set of footsteps, faint and barely discernible. Lacey.

Bug Eyes must have heard them too. He drew his pistol. Jude leaped toward the man and landed on his back, taking him down to the ground. Jude braced the man in place with his body despite his twisting and kicked to get away as he lay on his stomach.

"Lacey, I got him. Find something to tie him up with."

Bug Eyes groaned beneath Jude's weight. "Lacey?"

Jude looked up hearing more footsteps. Lacey stood over him. "I can't find anything."

"Get his coat off. We'll use the sleeves to time him up."

The man continued to struggle. Lacey ripped fabric and handed pieces to Jude. They tied his feet and gagged him, as well.

Both of them jumped to their feet. Jude grabbed the man's gun. It was a different gun than the one he had dropped in the kitchen.

Headlights glared at them from the road. George was getting desperate if he was taking the van out. Of course, if he mowed them down with it and then got rid of it and their bodies, the evidence left behind would not be substantial.

They took off running across the golf course which was still covered in snow. George lumbered toward them in the van.

Though the snow slowed George down, they would be no match for him on foot. They circled back around to the brick building where the pool was.

They ran around to the far side of the building and pressed against it. The van made a rumbling noise as it made its way across the snow toward them. Then he heard it. Wheels spinning. George had gotten bogged down in the melting snow and mud.

Jude gripped the gun. "Now's our chance. I'll go get him."

"I hope he's not armed," she said. "I'm going around the other side."

Jude crouched and moved along the building until he reached a corner where he could peer out. George had gotten out of the car and was stomping toward the swimming pool building.

It didn't look like he was holding a gun.

Jude listened to the sound of the approaching footsteps, waiting for the right moment.

The footsteps slowed down. Then stopped.

Jude's heart pounded.

Was George trying to figure out where Jude had gone? Or did he know and was waiting to jump him?

Taking in a breath Jude angled around the building and lifted the gun. "Hands up, George. It's over." George was maybe five feet away.

"You got me," George said. But he didn't raise his hands.

Jude tensed.

"But not really. I gave that gun to my associate when he lost his in the kitchen. I happen to know it has no bullets. We were in a hurry. I figured a gun pointed at you would be enough to stop you."

Was he bluffing? Jude pulled the trigger. Nothing happened.

Fear pierced Jude's heart as George lunged toward him, but then crumpled to the ground.

Lacey stood behind him holding a golf club that she had used to hit George on the head.

"Where did you find that?"

"In the outside garbage can by the pool. Someone must have been frustrated with it and tossed it."

"Give me the golf club. I'll watch him. You run over to that stuck van and find something to tie him up with."

Lacey returned a moment later. "All I could find were the cords they use to plug things in."

George stirred and groaned but didn't try to sit up.

Lacey tied George up and helped him into a sitting position.

"I'm going to need George's phone to call the police."

Lacey searched his coat pockets and made the call. "The police are five minutes away. They picked up that other guy based on the description the farmer gave. He ran a red light. They've been looking for us ever since we didn't make it to the sheriff's office."

Jude leaned close to George. "I want to know. If you wanted to keep your hands clean of the kidnapping, why even be in Montana at all? You might as well tell me. It's over for you."

"The ransom had to be in cash. After Reed took his cut, I needed that money to cover a debt before my wife found out. The snow-storm trapped me there. My wife couldn't get the ransom to my associate until the storm cleared. I met Dale. I saw how desperate he was for money. I got him to help me."

Exhausted, they both slumped down on the ground.

They sat with their shoulders touching. "I'm not a washed-up cop, you know," Jude said to George. "I'm a good detective and I'm thinking about going back on the force."

"Really?" Lacey said.

"When I almost died in that avalanche, I realized I needed to start living again. I cut people out of my life. I gave up on the job I loved. It's like I've been treading water for the last ten years."

"I know the feeling. That's not living and it's not what God wants for anyone. After my family died, I think I didn't want to risk lov-ing someone ever again," she said.

Jude's hand was resting on his knee. She reached over and placed her hand on top of his. The gesture made him believe that she was feeling the same way he was.

He twisted his hand around so he could squeeze hers. "Maybe I can find a cop job in Montana."

Her voice filled with affection. "I'd like that, Jude. Maybe I can get a job that doesn't involve moving all the time, put down roots somewhere."

They could not say much else with George glaring at them, but he had a feeling they were going to be spending more time together…if she felt the same way about him that he felt about her.

The flashing lights of several law enforcement vehicles brought a sense of relief for him.

Lacey let out a breath.

Hours later, they sat in the sheriff's office in Garnet. George and his accomplices were locked in jail cells.

Once they'd given their statements, the sheriff pushed his chair away from the desk. "When you two didn't show up, we went out looking for you. Took a while to put things together. Call from a farmer about two guys in a van acting suspicious. Still, I don't know that we would have found you if you hadn't phoned once the van gave highway patrol the slip."

They thanked the sheriff and stepped outside, bathed by the early morning light.

"I'm glad that's over," Lacey said. She stared into Jude's eyes. "So what happens now...to us?"

He touched her cheek and pulled her into a hug. "What say we both get jobs in the same town and maybe work on building a life together? I love you, Lacey."

She pulled back from the hug. Her eyes filled with warmth. "I love you too."

"Well, then." He leaned in and kissed her. He pulled back and touched her cheek, gazing at her. "I could stand a lifetime of kisses like that from you."

"Me too." Lacey wrapped her arms around Jude and he swung her around and then set her down.

"Here's to being alive again. With you," Jude said. "I don't know where all this is going but if we do end up married, let's honeymoon at the Davenport Hotel."

They both laughed.

* * * * *

*If you enjoyed this story,
look for* Wilderness Secrets *and*
In Too Deep *by Sharon Dunn.*

Dear Reader

Thank you for going on the exciting and dangerous suspense journey that Jude and Lacey experienced. While they were running for their lives, they were also making a discovery that they had not really been living at all. After the life-altering tragedies that both of them faced, it is normal to shut down and maybe even feel lost and hopeless for a time. With God's love though, I think we are meant to journey to a place of abundance and joy. Having faced some difficulties in my own life, I understand about living life on autopilot. Been there, done that, they make a T-shirt for it. I am by nature a pessimist. But I believe that we find healing and the full life God promises when we take risk, choose to love and walk in gratitude. God has so much for us.

Thank you,

Sharon Dunn

ReaderService.com has a new look!

We have refreshed our website and we want to share our new look with you. Head over to ReaderService.com and check it out!

On ReaderService.com, you can:

- Try 2 free books from any series
- Access risk-free special offers
- View your account history & manage payments
- Browse the latest Bonus Bucks catalog

Don't miss out!

If you want to stay up-to-date on the latest at the Reader Service and enjoy more Harlequin content, make sure you've signed up for our monthly News & Notes email newsletter. Sign up online at ReaderService.com.

RS19